THE REBEL

THE REBEL

BY HESTER BURTON

Illustrated by Victor G. Ambrus

THOMAS Y. CROWELL COMPANY   *New York*

First published in the United States of America in 1972
Copyright © 1971 by Hester Burton
All rights reserved. Except for use in a review,
the reproduction or utilization of this work in
any form or by any electronic, mechanical, or
other means, now known or hereafter invented,
including xerography, photocopying, and recording,
and in any information storage and retrieval
system is forbidden without the written permission
of the publisher.
Manufactured in the United States of America
L. C. Card 71-181829
ISBN 0-690-69010-X
1 2 3 4 5 6 7 8 9 10

Contents

For
ROBIN and SOPHIE

I

November the Fifth, 1788

"I don't want to go," muttered Stephen, as he stood at the kitchen window and stared out at the dreary dawn.

"But you *promised*," whispered Catherine in a frenzy of exasperation.

"I could lock myself in my room."

"No, you couldn't. They'd come knocking at your door, bullying you to go with us. And then . . ."

And then?

He sighed, knowing the truth. His great anger would burst out of him. And God knows what abuse he might not heap on his uncles and their heartless Centenary Celebrations. Catherine's gala day would be ruined from the start.

He stared out again at the driving rain.

"I'll get as wet as an otter," he grumbled, turning back for a last warm at the fire.

She went on cutting him great wedges of bread and cheese. She was sure of him now. He would keep his word. She and Martha could enjoy the great day.

He watched her gloomily, waiting for her to finish. She was barefoot, still in her nightdress, smiling to herself. Heavens! he thought, that the wearing of muslins and a new bonnet should mean so much to a girl! He was disgusted by her happiness. Ashamed of it. Had she not the wits to see that the whole thing was a mockery? If it were not that she was his sister—and that he was fond of her—he'd be damned if he'd go shuffling off furtively

1

like this before they were all up. He'd stay and tell his two pestilential uncles that they and the Duke of Ullswater and the landed gentry of Westmorland were a dishonest pack of hypocrites—and have done with it.

Excited, still smiling, her work done, Catherine ran to the window, unlatched the casement, and leaned far out to scan the full stretch of sky between the two ranges of hills.

"Look!" she whispered eagerly. "There's a rim of light westward behind the pike. It'll be fine before eleven."

She turned back into the room, snatched up the bread and cheese, and hurried him to the threshold.

"Take your hat and the shepherd's cloak," she said. "You'll be all right when the wind dies down. You'll like it up there. You know you will."

A loud creaking started up in the house behind them.

"Quick!" she said hoarsely, thrusting the food into his hands. "Quick! Or it'll be too late!"

She stood watching him impatiently as he loped off across the farmyard, longing for him to be safely away before his escape was discovered.

"Where is he going?" asked a voice at her side.

She looked round, half angry, half guilty.

It was Martha, her schoolfriend, in her nightdress.

"To the hills," she replied shortly. "Why did you get up?"

"I wondered where you were. It was cold in that great bed without you."

Martha looked over Catherine's shoulder at the lonely figure trudging up the hill path in the driving rain.

"Isn't Stephen coming with us to watch the processions?"

"No."

Once out of sight of the farm, he sat down on a rock beside the brook, made a rough tent against the rain with his shepherd's cloak, and flung chippings of granite into an eddying pool.

A hundred years of freedom, indeed! Freedom from what? Hunger? Disease? Injustice? Death? What freedom had the old soldier, maimed by the wars, begging his bread from door to door? What freedom had any *poor* man in England? Or any woman or child? What freedom had orphans—like Catherine and Josh and himself—left to the care of unloving relations? Poor Catherine! he thought savagely, aiming a stone at a rowan sapling growing from a crack in a rock in the middle of the brook. Poor, silly girl, walking with her schoolfriend down to Camberstock in all her finery to rejoice that she was free. What freedom could *she* ever know?

He rose at last, shook himself free from his stiffness, and started climbing up the brook towards the tarn, leaping from rock to glistening rock, bound for the upper light, for—above and ahead of him—stretched Catherine's rim of clear sky, now as broad and as blue as a sweep of the sea.

By nine o'clock, the last of the storm clouds had swept away eastward, and he had come out from the defile onto the broad back of Blenby Moor. Here, he sat down under a holly brake on a slope commanding a wide view not only of the surrounding hills and dales, but also of the broad Camber valley and the three pack-horse roads that wound through the hills down to Camberstock. From this vantage point, he watched the morning grow, bathing his native hills with an unpromised splendor. The November sunlight glowed in the tawny bracken farther down the slopes, glinted in every stream and runlet, and caught in every droplet hanging from every grass blade close at hand, so that each way he turned he was dazzled and enchanted by the million refractions of its rays. The artist in him that could not draw and the poet in him that was wordless, were swept with joy. For a magic moment, he forgot the injustices of life.

And then his eye caught the valley road to Camberstock. He stared at it idly at first, watching a few early travelers making for the town. As the minutes passed, the stray farmer and his family were followed by another and another, until now as he looked the road was filled with people. He stood up in astonishment and stared at them. He had never seen such crowds of countryfolk before. It was worse than Fair Week. Far worse. There were ladies in carriages, gentlemen on horseback, poor folk astride donkeys and mules, charcoal burners and men from slate quarries striding along in their Sunday boots. And, as his eyes swept the quiet hills above, he saw that shepherds and peddlers and pack-men were coming down along the pack roads that wound through the rocks. The whole of Westmorland was emptying itself into the town for the stupid celebrations. He stood in the early sunlight, glaring down at the world of his childhood in bitter, raging disbelief.

The poor, the wronged, the dispossessed were bent on rejoicing, too.

At eleven o'clock, the bells of St. Kentigern's Church rang out. To Catherine, standing beside Martha in the Clappergate, the joy of their peal seemed as breathtaking as a great flight of swans.

The great day had begun.

The bells were the signal for the processions to set out from the castle gate. In a few minutes, they would hear the bands and the steady clop of the horses' feet. The ceremony of thanksgiving was upon them. Whatever Stephen said, had they not reason to be thankful? A hundred years of liberty. A hundred years today since Prince William of Orange had landed in England and put an end to the tyranny of kings!

Now they could hear the blare of the trumpets and the rattle of the kettledrums through the paean of the bells.

"They're coming," said Martha. "We'll see them in a minute."

The crowds lining the route farther up the street were bursting into cheers. They could see the men taking off their hats and waving them in the air. In the houses over their heads, people were standing at their windows waving orange scarves and shouting "Huzzah! Huzzah!" Catherine felt dizzy with joy. Bells. Trumpets. Cheers. She had never heard such an intoxicating din.

"Here they come!" shouted a tradesman standing beside them.

"Where? Where?" she cried. "Oh, Martha, I can't see!"

For, at the approach of the procession, her uncles and her aunt, who had been sitting on the bench immediately in front of them, suddenly all decided to stand up.

"It's only the constables," Martha tried to console her. "They're marching two by two, carrying their staves."

It was all right for Martha. She was tall.

"Don't look at me," Catherine shot back. "Look at the procession and tell me what you see."

She was completely walled in by the throng.

"And now comes Mr. Pickersgill's Revolution Club," Martha reported. "They're marching four by four—each gentleman bearing a white wand with a blue and orange knot tied at its tip. And there's a flag, Catherine. A gentleman, leading the company, is carrying a blue and orange flag!"

"Has it . . . has it got a motto?"

"Yes, it has," replied Martha excitedly. " 'THE GLORIOUS REVOLUTION, 1688' and underneath the figure of Liberty crowning Britannia with a laurel wreath."

"Oh, I wish I could see it. I wish I could," cried Catherine, trying to gulp back her disappointment.

"And so you shall, lass," roared a voice behind her.

And before she knew what was happening she felt herself lifted up out of the throng and perched high on a broad shoulder.

"Hold tight, child," laughed the Camberstock wheelwright. "Clutch on to my hair."

She gasped her thanks and her astonished delight, for seated now far above the heads of the crowd, she could see right down the length of the processions—past the four Revolution Clubs with their different flags, past the Westmorland Militia Band, to the Duke of Ullswater's coach and six.

The band broke into "Rule Britannia." The crowds roared. The apprentices on the Assembly Room steps bellowed out the refrain. And the boys running along the roof ridges let off volley upon volley of firecrackers.

The processions were now winding into the marketplace. From where they stood they could clearly see the blue and orange cockades bobbing up and down on the Duke of Ullswater's black horses as they clattered up the street. At the approach of His Grace, the crowd bowed and curtsied. Catherine, perched up high, stared down on the scene entranced. Then, immediately below her, off came her uncles' beavers and down went Martha and Aunt Biddy in the curtsies they had practiced last night.

In the carriage, she saw the wizened face of an old man, smiling thinly.

Then, her eyes wandered. They traveled across the marketplace, thronged with shopkeepers and farmers and saddlers and shepherds, all baring their heads and making their bows, and fastened upon one solitary, upright figure, standing as indomitable as a mountain, his hat jammed tight upon his head.

"Martha!" she gasped, white with shock. "Martha!"

She let go the wheelwright's hair and slithered to the ground.

"What's the matter?" exclaimed Martha and the wheelwright together.

But Catherine could only shake her head and stammer:

"I . . . I . . . felt dizzy . . . sitting up there."

Stephen had *promised* to keep away. Not to flaunt his foolish, rebellious views. And there he was—standing in the very middle of the marketplace, his great hat pulled down hard on his head— a landmark as conspicuous as the beacon on Camberstock Hill.

"Oh, Martha," she said. "We're going to have such an awful end to this happy day!"

For Stephen, it was an even worse end to an unhappy one.

Bewildered beyond measure to see so many shepherds and peddlers and packmen coming down from the hills to watch the gentry at their foolish parade, he had left his holly brake and followed them down into Camberstock. Here was a mystery that he could not understand. He knew these people. He had known them all his life—known them as only a boy could know them who had walked whole days by their side. Though they were poor, they were not abject. Though they could neither read nor write, they were not ignorant. They were tough; harsh; craggy. He loved them. He loved their dignity and independence. He could not bear to think that such men—through patriotism, or because of a vulgar show of pomp—might be fooled by this mockery of a celebration. For what freedom had the last hundred years brought to *them?* Those fine gentlemen in the processions had enclosed their commons, pulled down their cottages, felled their woods—despoiled and stolen their native hills. Were they trooping down, perhaps, not to rejoice in the centenary but to protest against these wrongs? Was Camberstock in for an uproar? He quickened his pace.

As he stood in the marketplace, he knew that they were fooled. They had come down from the hills not to fight for their rights but to gape and cheer—and, afterwards, to get drunk in the Camberstock inns. Free hogsheads of ale provided by the Duke! Who could resist such an invitation to rejoice?

Greatly disappointed in the dignity of man, he wandered wretchedly about the streets all afternoon, watching the dalesmen gorging themselves with food and dousing their native pride with the Duke's largess, marveling sadly that human nature could sell its birthright for so little. New bonnets and ribbons for the girls; beef and beer for the men; church bells and drumbeats and banners for all—blessed by a thin-lipped smile!

But worse was to come.

By nightfall, the drunkenness turned to brawling. Not brawling against the dishonest Duke, with his cruel evictions and his
mantraps. But brawling against Stephen *himself!*

"Thet's 'im!" bawled a tipsy voice, as he entered the inn yard at
the back of the *King's Head*. "Thet's 'im as wouldn' bare 'is
'ead t' Duke!"

"Knock 'is 'at off on 'im now!" laughed another.

An empty mug was pitched at his head.

He ducked.

"And why should I bow before the Duke?" he shouted at them. "Why should *you?* Is he the poor man's friend?"

"Troublemaker!" bellowed a man from the shadows behind him.

And, suddenly, a blow on the back of the head sent him sprawling on the cobbles.

"He robs you! He cheats you!" he shouted, as he tried to pick himself up.

"Democrat!" bawled a great lout close at hand. "Take that for yer pains!"

And a pewter mug struck his temple.

He was down now. Truly down—with the blood streaming into his eyes. And, knowing him to be down, the drunken inn yard came about him with its boots.

Up at the farm at Town End, Catherine was in great wretchedness. Her uncles had just come home with news of a brawl. It was ten o'clock. And Stephen had not returned. She sat with her friend Martha in the darkness of her bedroom, staring out miserably at the screaming rockets bursting softly in the sky.

"It's those hogsheads of ale," said Martha gently. "They're not used to so much."

But Catherine shook her head. It was Stephen. She was sure it was Stephen. He drove people mad with his crazy ideas.

Stephen had killed the bright day—for others, besides herself, had seen his insult to the Duke. It had blanched Aunt Biddy's cheeks, blighted the ladies' luncheon at the *George,* and brought thunder about her ears on her uncles' return.

"Catherine, your brother has shamed us!" Uncle Fletcher had stormed at her. "He's brought disgrace upon us all!"

"We've raised a cuckoo, Biddy," Uncle Matthew had hiccupped. "A bastard'y young cuckoo in the nest!"

"He deserves a good drubbing," Uncle Fletcher had raged.

Three rockets shot up in a handful into the night sky and burst silently into flower.

"Don't fret," murmured Martha. "He's come to no harm. He'll soon be home."

Catherine prayed she was right. And two minutes later, as though in answer to her prayer, there was a faint creaking on the stair.

"It's Stephen!" she whispered, running quickly to the door to let him in.

He came to them in the darkness. He saw the faint glimmer of their faces and their pale muslins—heard the quick intake of their breath.

"Stephen!" exclaimed Catherine.

"You are hurt!" said her friend.

"It's nothing!" he hissed angrily. "Get me water and a cloth."

The girl that he hardly knew lit a candle. And Catherine cried out:

"Your eye! Stephen, your eye!"

They came about him then with the bedroom jug and a towel.

"I fell," he muttered.

"Falls do not tear sleeves out of coats," murmured Catherine's friend, as she began stanching his wound.

"Very well," he snapped at her. "They set upon me—six of them—in the inn yard."

"But *why?*" cried Catherine.

"Does it matter why?"

He felt broken. It was only his anger that saved his pride.

"It needs a stitch," murmured the stranger. "You should go to the surgeon."

"No," he answered impatiently. "Bind it up with a strip of cloth. It'll heal."

He could not bear that anyone should probe deeper into his hurt, see his bruised ribs, guess his battered hopes. He could not bear to be reminded of what had happened to him at the back of the *King's Head*. And, because he could not bear to think of it, he must think of something else, *do* something else—not slink like a whipped dog to his kennel.

"My uncles?" he asked suddenly, as the girls were binding up his forehead. "Did they see me in the marketplace?"

Catherine nodded her head.

"They are angry?"

"Very."

He grinned. Suddenly he felt better.

"Go up and get my other coat," he told his sister. "I'll beard the old fools tonight."

"No!" cried Catherine, clinging to him. "Uncle Matthew's drunk."

"Your Uncle Fletcher's very angry with you," pleaded the stranger.

Intoxicated by his own bravado, he twisted himself free from them both, and, leaving them clutching his tattered coat, banged down the stairs in his shirtsleeves.

"Tonight," he shouted back at them in triumph. "It must be *tonight!*"

Dear God! Why had they not stopped him? Catherine groaned in anguish later that night. Why had they not flung themselves on him, grappled with him—made it bodily impossible for him to have driven Uncle Fletcher into such a fury?

Instead, having failed to stop him, they let fall his wretched coat, crept halfway down the stairs in his wake, and stood there, listening—sick at heart—to the uproar in the parlor below.

"Why should I honor such a man?" Stephen was shouting.

"Because he is your better!" snarled Uncle Fletcher.

"*Better!* Do I beggar my tenants? Do I drive them out of their rightful homes?"

"Peace, you fool."

"Do I pull a man's roof down about his ears? And for what reason? Because I want his fields for my paddock! For my *racehorses!*"

"Baldry's cottage was the Duke's. His fields were the Duke's. The Duke was but taking back his own."

"His own? And who gave it him?"

"It 'longed t'his fayther, you stoopid boy," bawled Uncle Matthew.

"Baldry's father worked Baldry's holding before *him*," flashed Stephen. "And Baldry's grandfather and great-grandfather before that. It was not honest—not *just*—to treat him so."

"The Duke has the law on his side," whipped out Uncle Fletcher.

"The law! And who made the law? Your precious Duke, I do not doubt!"

"It is the law of *England!*" shouted Uncle Fletcher.

"The law of England's *rich*, Uncle, to beggar England's *poor*."

"Dear Heavens!" gasped Catherine.

Stephen had gone too far! Much too far.

Uncle Fletcher was a lawyer. And he was the Duke's agent.

"Tee hee," guffawed the tipsy Uncle Matthew. "That's had 'un, brother! That's gi'en 'un a proper knock."

"You young whelp," roared Uncle Fletcher, stung to rage. "You're . . . you're a renegade to your class."

"And what class is that, Uncle?" Stephen mocked.

Catherine went scarlet with grief.

Stephen had now gone beyond all forgiveness—for their father had been a gentleman, far above their mother and her brothers in birth. Their father, ruined by his own folly, had once owned his own country seat.

"Get out of our house," bellowed Uncle Fletcher. "Get out, I say. We've done with you."

"That's it, nevvy," agreed Uncle Matthew, giving a drunken belch. "We're tired of you . . . sick and tired o' the whole pack of you."

Catherine turned to Martha in utter bewilderment. Herself? Josh? What had *they* ever done to make her uncles tired of them?

"Why? What have the others done?"

Stephen sounded suddenly appalled.

"Nay, Catherine's a good lass. She c'n stay an' welcome. But the other's to go—ain't that so, Fletcher?"

"But Josh is at school!" protested Stephen. "He can't bother you here. He's got years yet at school."

"I think not," said Uncle Fletcher curtly. "Your brother Joshua is not clever. We are sending him to sea."

"No! Not to *sea!*" burst out Catherine.

Josh hated the sea.

"But you *can't!*" exclaimed Stephen. "He's . . . he's only a boy."

Josh was fourteen.

"We can and will," replied Uncle Fletcher coldly.

"Your Uncle Parkin 'a' spoke for 'un," explained Uncle Matthew.

"Uncle Richard?"

"Captain Parkin says that if your brother does well on his first voyage," continued Uncle Fletcher, "then he will take him on the China run. Joshua is not easy to place in the world. It is too good a chance for us to miss."

Catherine's heart ached, for she knew that he was right.

Poor Josh was a fool at his books. And—what was almost as bad—he stammered terribly whenever he felt shy.

"As for yourself, sir," rasped Uncle Fletcher, closing the matter. "You will go back to Ellenhead tomorrow. We will pay for your lodging with Mrs. Mossop until it is time for you to go up to Oxford. You are not to return here—not till your tutors and professors have taught you the folly of your ways."

Catherine gasped. She could hardly believe her ears. They were sending him back to *school!* Stephen! Almost a grown man!

The two girls heard him stride out of the parlor by the other door, bang through the kitchen, and let himself out into the yard.

"Leave him," whispered Martha, restraining Catherine from running out to him.

Hours later, he came up to them.

"Catherine," he whispered, tapping softly on the bedroom door.
She ran to let him in.
"Stephen."
"Hush," he muttered. "Don't wake the house."
She pulled him into the room.
"I'm going back to Ellenhead," he said dully.
"We know. We heard."
"And Josh is to go to sea."
The tears began crawling down Catherine's cheeks.
"I know. We heard it all."

As he stood there in the darkness, his figure became slowly distinct. They saw the whiteness of his shirt and the bandage round his head.

"I cannot wait till morning," he said. "I am off tonight."
"Tonight?"
'The moon rises in an hour. It will light me on the hills."
"But your clothes?"

"Send them after me—by the carrier."

He told them that he could not bear to see his uncles in the morning. He would leave immediately—leave them to a barren triumph.

"And what about *me?*" Catherine burst out, hurt and angry—knowing herself abandoned.

He gazed at her blankly, lost in his own wretchedness.

"You have a friend," he said at last, glancing absently at Martha.

As he climbed Crag Hill towards the old Roman road, he put Catherine's small troubles behind him. He had worse of his own.

They were not his banishment from his uncles' home; he cared nothing for his uncles. They were not his going to Ellenhead; he had always been happy at school. They were not even the manner of his going; that was but a hurt to his vanity. They were the terrible words that had been spoken to him as he lay bleeding on the cobblestones in the inn yard.

A man had bent down and spat in his face.

"What do the likes o' *you* know about the mis'ries o' the poor?" he had jeered at him.

It was a familiar voice—the voice of a shepherd: a man who had befriended him as a small boy and who had once fashioned him a crook.

The pain of it tore at him afresh.

The mountain track was steep. As he sweated and panted up the height, straining his eyes for the rabbit holes and the rocks and the sleeping sheep, a dullness crept over the throbbing cut and his bruised ribs. He was scrambling up now, grabbing the cold grass in his hands. And now, at last, he was at the top, standing on the old road.

He turned and looked all about him—up at the clouds hurrying high over his head, across at the dim diffusion of the moonlight behind Skelcrag Mountain, and then down below his feet at the folds of darkness that hid Camberstock and its inn yard.

And then, he found himself laughing. Laughing at himself. What *did* he know about the sufferings of the poor?

2

Josh

At the end of morning classes Josh Parkin ran out into Ellenhead town square with his bread and cheese in one hand and Uncle Fletcher's unopened letter in the other. He hated his uncle and he was sure that his letter boded no good, so—looking all about him to make certain that he was not followed—he slipped down by the lakeside and hid himself in a clump of willows before breaking the seal.

This is what he read:

Dear Joshua,

Seeing that you will be fifteen next month, and learning from your master that you are never likely to make even a tolerable scholar in the Latin language, your Uncle Parkin and myself think it best that you leave Ellenhead at Christmas and go at once to sea. There is a trading ship, the *Orion,* Captain Fulford, bound for New York and the West Indies, sailing from Liverpool early in the New Year. Your Uncle Parkin, by using his influence, has secured a voyage for you with the Captain, who will see that you are instructed in the business of the sea.

You are aware of the straitened circumstances in which your father left his three children and of the great sacrifices made by myself and my brother Matthew in taking you all into our home and in husbanding your very slender resources so that they should provide Stephen and Catherine and yourself with an education commensurate with your breeding. These resources are nearly at

an end. It seems to us best, therefore, that such money as remains in your father's estate should be used to pay for your brother's expenses at Oxford. If he works well and obtains a college fellowship, then he can win preferment in the Church and will be in a position to provide a home for himself and Catherine until such time as your sister should marry.

As for yourself, a sea career offers the best promise for a boy without an inheritance and without those natural gifts which would distinguish him in the genteeler professions of the Church and the Law. If you can prove your worth—and, my dear boy, give evidence of a greater energy and concentration than you have hitherto shown—then you have powerful family friends in the East India Company who may well be persuaded to help you to posts at once honorable to a gentleman and profitable to his fortune.

> I remain, your dutiful uncle,
> Fletcher Birkett.

P.S. Catherine bids me tell you that you need new shirts. She will have these ready for you before you go to sea, if you will send her the measurements by the carrier on his return from Ellenhead. She bids you measure particularly the *outside* arm length from cuff to shoulder and also the *thickness* of your neck.

Josh flung the letter from him, appalled by its dreadful common sense and obscurely angry with Catherine for fussing about his shirts. The sea. He hated the sea. It was a barren waste. A monster. A death. And all that Catherine could think of was the length of his arms! Had she no heart? Did she not care? He picked up the letter and plodded through it again, searching desperately for a hint of escape—but found none. He was too stupid to stay longer at school, it said. And there was no money to buy him a farm. He shuddered. It was not just the sea that he feared but the terrible life that went with it.

His thoughts drifted back to last summer and to his coming upon James Askrigg, home from sea, leaning against the wall of his father's cottage and gazing down, sick at heart, on the meadows of long grass far below him.

"Thet's better'n all t' seven seas," James had sighed.

They had sat on in silence, Josh chewing a grass stem.

"Don't you never go to sea, Josh," the unhappy sailor had begged him. "It's no life for a dalesman—not after this."

And his eyes had swept the whole peaceful scene from the swaying grasses up to the top of Longthwaite Hill where, high on the skyline, a shepherd was moving slowly along a mountain path, calling to his dog in short, harsh cries which had come down to them in the stillness.

"Wh-what's s-so dreadful about it?" he had asked.

The floggings, the drunkenness, the filth, and the cold, had come the grim reply.

"And that's not the worst of it."

"Wh-what's the w-worst?"

"It's that no-spot, Josh, *no-spot* on shipboard is a man left to be by hisself!"

Never to be alone! Ever!

Sitting now on the shore of Ellenwater with Uncle Fletcher's horrible letter in his hand, Josh was briefly swept with an un-speakable panic.

Then he remembered that he was not a child but almost a man. And a Parkin at that. If the sea was his lot in life, then he had better run down the road to his lodging and get Mrs. Mossop to measure the thickness of his neck before the school bell rang for the afternoon's declamations and before the carrier returned from Ellendale on his way back to Camberstock. If the sea was the best he was good for, then that was that.

As he emerged from the willow clump, grim with resolve, he caught sight of a familiar figure loping down the pack road from Ambleside. It was Stephen. It was Stephen's mountain gait. But what was he doing coming back to Ellenhead? And why did he have that white thing round his head?

He ran towards him.

"S-Stephen," he shouted.

His brother raised his hand in welcome and loped towards him without changing his pace.

"Wh-what's happened?" he shouted again, recognizing the white thing as a bandage. "Are you hurt?"

Stephen grinned and shook his head.

"Wh-what's happened?" he stammered, as he stood—out of breath—at his brother's side.

"Got in a brawl," Stephen laughed. "In Camberstock . . . night of the celebrations."

"A b-brawl?" Josh exclaimed, greatly impressed.

"Drunken louts. It's nothing. How's school?"

School? What a stupid question! It was just itself.

"And Mr. Walkinshaw?"

"All right. Qu-quite all right."

His words came out in an uncontrolled rush. Mr. Walkinshaw was quite another matter. Josh liked him. They both liked him. The master of Ellenhead School was the kindest grown-up Josh had ever met.

Then, still puzzled, he looked searchingly at his brother.

"S-Stephen, why have you come b-back?"

Stephen regarded the gangling boy and sensed how it must seem to him for his brother to come striding in from the outside world—a hero, a man free at last from the discipline of school.

He decided to tell him only half the truth.

"I quarreled with our uncles," he said with a laugh. "And since there was no peace in the house, I decided to come back to Mrs. Mossop's until it's time for me to go up to Oxford."

"B-but what will you *do?*" stammered the astonished Josh.

It was nearly two months to the New Year and the Hilary Term.

"Read, walk, fish . . . do a bit of poaching," he grinned. "And come to visit you at school."

As if in answer to the word, the great bell in the school belfry clanged across the dale.

"My God!" burst out Josh, suddenly brought back to Uncle Fletcher's letter and his hateful plight.

Mrs. Mossop, he stammered. The shirts. Catherine wanted the length of his arms.

Stephen seized his shoulders.

"What are you talking about?"

"I'm g-g-going to s-sea," he shouted over the clamor of the bell, as he started running back towards the town.

Stephen ran at his side.

"Do you mind dreadfully?"

"Y-yes. I do."

They came to a halt together at the stone stile.

"You may make your fortune," Stephen panted, trying to comfort him.

"May I?"

"They say Uncle Richard will be a rich man if his present venture succeeds."

"D-do *you* want to be rich?" Josh tossed at him, as he jumped down into the road.

"Not particularly."

"J-just as well," he shouted over the mounting din of the bell. "Uncle F-Fletcher says you've got to be a p-p-parson."

And he fled pell-mell down the street towards Mrs. Mossop's cottage.

It was the afternoon of the declamations. Every boy in the Upper School had to stand up and recite verses from a poem of his own choice. Some chose passages from Homer, others from Virgil, while one burst into Henry V's harangue before Agincourt.

Poor Josh had chosen the shortest and easiest poem that he could find. Up he stood and stammered out Alexander Pope's famous "Ode on Solitude":

> *Happy the man, whose wish and care*
> *A few paternal acres bound,*
> *Content to breathe his native air,*
> *In his own ground.*

Stephen, listening from the seat in the great window, was swept with a terrible pity for his brother. Poor devil! Poor devil! he thought. Josh—like the man in the poem—was asking so little from life: merely to stay here in Westmorland and shepherd his own sheep. He wanted only a hut, a fold, and a hillside.

> *Whose herds with m-milk, whose f-f-fields with b-bread,*
> *Whose f-f-flocks supply him with attire . . .*

The boy soldiered on, getting redder in the face and stammering worse with each verse until, finding himself safely launched on the final quatrain, he took courage and came romping home like a young horse making straight for his stable. Having come to the end, he sat down bang on his bench and was thankful to be heard no more.

Meanwhile, to Stephen, after pity had come anger: a terrible anger against his elders. By what right had his three uncles the power to banish Josh from his native dale and pack him off to sea? What justice was there anywhere for the young? On and on he raged inside himself while the recitations continued and the cadences of Horace and Ovid and Sidney and Spenser fell about his ears, now piped and now growled by the boys of Ellenhead. Why, for pity's sake, should Josh have to be a sailor and himself a parson and Catherine get married off to the first bidder to save them all her keep? Why were people fettered by custom and tradition? By money—or the lack of it? By an older generation established in its power? Pray God, he ranted to himself—for he was certainly not praying—pray God there came a time when there was an end to one man's dominion over another; when the poor and the young and all women were free. When . . .

"Stephen . . ."

It was the master, Mr. Walkinshaw. By his patient smile, he had clearly called his name before.

Now he spoke again. For the sake of former times, he asked, would Stephen like to join in the school exercise and recite some poem to them that he liked?

Yes. Stephen would.

He leaped to his feet and, without a moment's hesitation, plunged headlong into Satan's mighty speech in *Paradise Lost* in which the fallen angel addresses his colleagues lying on the burning lake in hell:

> *What though the field be lost?*
> *All is not lost . . .*

Josh, who had been staring out of the window at the view of Ellencrag Mountain, rising sharp and grim on the far side of the lake, and lost in a dream of another poaching night with Stephen, was startled by his brother's voice, northern and rocky as the scene outside, hurling defiance at the Great Dictator of the Universe.

"Y-you made it sound as though Satan was right," he protested as they walked back together to Mrs. Mossop's cottage in the twilight.

"So he was," came the cheerful reply.

A week later Josh had his wish.

He and Stephen climbed out of their bedroom window by way of Mrs. Mossop's apple tree, crept through the mist-swathed garden, and set out for a night's poaching in the hills.

Back he was with his brother—not boy to his man, but comrades.

It began to drizzle, and the raindrops clung to his hair and eyebrows and brushed softly against his cheeks. It was the kind of night he loved. The earth was full of fresh smells, and the light from the moon, coming faintly through the passing cloud, caught dimly in the glistening ferns and the wet stones in the road. In half an hour they would be up on the moor above the cloud, and there the moon would be mirrored clear and bright in the tarn, and its light would bathe in glory the wide sweep of heather and the stretches of boggy grass and the clumps of moss where the foolish woodcock ran between the white pebbles set by the boys to lead the birds into their snares.

"It's too early for them," Stephen had grumbled the evening before. "They don't come till next month."

"A f-few may have f-flown in," he had urged. "You n-never know."

He had been desperate for this night's sport.

And Stephen, suddenly seeing the wastes of ocean that lay ahead of his brother, had relented and grinned.

"Why not? But we'll not take the springes—just a sack for the birds we find caught."

As they climbed up the packhorse road to the pass, the murmur of countless small streams wending their way valleyward through the coarse grasses and over the stones on the hillside, came to them through the darkness. Now that they were walking up through the last torn wreaths of the low cloud, it was dank and cold, and Stephen was momentarily cut off from Josh by the heavy mist, so that he only knew that he was there by the sharp clump of his boots on the stones. The moon struggled clear for a second and then disappeared again. And then, at last, the wreaths of the cloud drifted away below their feet, and the moor in all its glory stretched radiant as a moonlit sea.

They stood together, gazing in fresh wonder at the unearthly beauty of this quiet world above the darkness.

Josh strode on at last—and then stopped in his tracks. He had heard the sudden, still, tearing sound of a woodcock rising from the feeding ground.

Stephen stopped short at his side.

"You were right," he breathed. "They have come."

Another whirring sound of wings broke the silence, and then another, and another. The two brothers stood, eager and breathless, watching the swift dodging flight of the birds as they skimmed off to the safety of the woods far below them in the dale.

Then, when the last bird had disappeared, and the silence had come back, Stephen ran out into the sea of heather.

"Come," he cried, seized with a wild laughter. "Let's free the rest of them caught in the snares!"

He had flung away the sack that he had been carrying and was crashing through the springy stems of the dead heather towards the plateau of grassy bog, shouting a mad halloo to the moonlit mountaintops.

Josh stood and watched him, appalled at the din he was making and dismayed at the end of their poaching.

Then, he plodded after him.

Stephen was far ahead by now, stooping to release a woodcock from a snare. Then he stood upright with the bird struggling in his grasp—a lone figure under the huge bowl of the sky.

Then, suddenly, he flung wide his arms.

" 'Rise from the ground like feather'd Mercury!' " he yelled triumphantly, as he shot the frightened creature into flight towards the stars.

"Damn him!" grumbled Josh. "That's good food."

Stephen was crazy. Just as crazy as he had always been.

Five weeks later, school broke up for the Christmas holidays.

Stephen and Mr. Walkinshaw wrung Josh's hand and told him to have courage, and then set off together over the Furness Hills

with their packs upon their backs to spend Christmas with the schoolmaster's mother in Greenburn.

It was a strange friendship, Josh thought, as he stood at the school gate watching the two of them climb the hill past the courthouse: strange not because Mr. Walkinshaw did not deserve his brother's affection, but because Stephen—with all his wildness—was considered to be worthy of Mr. Walkinshaw's. Grown-ups were very unexpected in the people they forgave.

Then, having made sure that his portmanteau, his skates, his fishing rod, and his Christmas present for Catherine were all safely stacked at his side, he turned round and stared miserably at the empty playground and at the barred windows of the Upper School, and cursed his Uncle Matthew for his tardiness in sending the cart to fetch him away. The other boys had left Ellenhead an hour ago. Some of them might even be home by now. And here he was, left awkwardly alone, with the townspeople staring at him as they crossed the square and wondering why he still remained.

He kept his back turned upon them and continued to gaze sadly at the smooth patch in the corner where he had played marbles long ago, then at the elm tree that he had climbed to the very top, then at the raised piece of ground in the middle where all the school fights had been fought. He smiled for a moment— for he had triumphed there. And then he felt glum again. He had been happy at Ellenhead. And now it was shut against him. It was all over. It was in the past.

And the future?

Josh suddenly shivered in the cold December air. God alone knew what the future held.

The stablehand from Town End came for him at last, and away they rattled over the rough road to Ambleside, trying to catch up with lost time on this shortest of days. But it was dusk as they wound down the long descent from the Kirkstone Pass, dark as they skirted the shores of Ullswater, and late at night when they bowled through Camberstock and took the rutted lane to the farm.

"Josh, you're here! You're here, at last," cried Catherine, running out into the yard.

He jumped down from the cart, and his sister flung her arms round him in an ecstasy of affection which—hidden from all eyes by the darkness—he was only too happy to receive. Yet, in the middle of their embrace, he stiffened and then pushed her roughly aside.

"What is it?" she exclaimed, bewildered.

From over her shoulder, he had caught sight of a stranger—a girl—who had just come out onto the kitchen threshold and was standing there, watching them, a lantern in her hand.

"It's only Martha," said Catherine, laughing. "Martha, this is Josh. Josh, this is Martha, my friend from school."

Scarlet in the face, Josh scowled at his sister's friend and then nodded her a curt greeting.

"I'll go and lay out the supper," said Martha, leaving them.

"The servants have gone to bed. We've got the kitchen to ourselves," said Catherine, chattering gaily to cover up the awkwardness.

As they pulled his portmanteau out of the back of the cart, she longed to tell Josh that Martha was not like other girls, but she could not think of suitable terms in which to describe her friend: terms that would not scare him worse than he was scared already.

"Don't worry," she said at last, picking up his fishing rod and skates. "Martha's not a bit clever—not like Phoebe Clapperton. She never laughs at one or makes one feel a fool."

The stranger was busying herself at the hearth when they entered the kitchen, and stayed there, her back turned to them, while Catherine took his coat, chafed his numb hands, and fussed over him joyfully as only Catherine could, while all the time pouring out the small news of the farm.

"Uncle Fletcher's in Carlisle on the Duke's business," she said, fetching him the jug of mulled ale. "And Uncle Matthew's asleep in the parlor with the livestock prices spread out over his face. And Aunt Biddy's gone up to bed. She's not well. She's not been well for months. And Martha and I—we've just discovered why."

"Why?" he asked absently, still dazed to be back in the world of home.

"She's going to have a *baby*."

"A b-b-baby," stammered the astonished Josh. "She's m-m-much too old!"

But it was true, all the same, Catherine went on. Aunt Biddy had told Mrs. Brownlow. And Mrs. Brownlow had told Martha's cousin. It was coming in the spring. In April, they thought. Very odd it was, after all these years.

It was worse than odd for poor Josh. He picked up his mug of ale quickly and buried his face in it, trying to hide from the others the final death of his hopes. For in the secret depths of his heart, he had always been sure that when Uncle Matthew died he would leave him this farm at Town End. He knew that Uncle Matthew did not like him any better than he liked Uncle Matthew; but they were both farmers by nature. And they were related. He was his uncle's sister's son. He and Stephen were his natural heirs . . . until . . . until this baby suddenly decided to be born.

"Here's your supper, Josh," said Martha, quietly slipping a plate of lamb stew and carrots in front of him.

The food smelled good—meaty and hot: a comfort to a cold body and battered hopes. As he ate it, he noticed that it had a special savor, compounded of thyme and marjoram and outdoor scents, that he had never met before in the cooking at Town End.

When he had finished it, he sat on, staring in silence at the ribbed graining of the kitchen table, thinking vaguely of the pleasant things women could do for a man and dazed anew at what the grown-up world was doing in sending him away to sea.

"Josh," said Martha quietly. "You're dreadfully tired. You look half asleep."

Catherine had finished with weeping for her two brothers. There was nothing she could do for Stephen. He was beyond her help. Indeed, she could not remember a time when he had ever been within it. He must make the best of Oxford—and Oxford of him. The wide world had to cope with him now—and he with it.

As for Josh, she had knitted him sea stockings and finished his shirts and packed the sea chest that Uncle Fletcher had brought back from Whitehaven. And now, there was nothing left but to make him happy in his last days at home.

The weather came to her rescue.

Those last days of the dying year were silver and pale gold to the very end. Hill and dale rang in the grip of an iron frost. The sun shone by day; and at night the moon rose in a sky pricked sharp with a thousand stars.

"*This* is what he'll remember," she told herself happily, as she and Martha and Josh wheeled round and round on the polished ice, the bare trees on the lakeshore shooting past behind them to the ringing hiss of their skates. "He'll take these lovely days with him to New York and Jamaica, and later—to Canton. He'll remember how the sky looks . . . and the mountains . . . and the frozen waterfall . . . and the ferns all stiff and spangled with the frost."

She was quite wrong.

It was Martha's quiet face, flushed from skating, peeping out from a dark fur bonnet, that Josh took away with him to the seven seas.

3

Stephen

For the first few weeks, Stephen was bewitched by Oxford. The towers, the spires, the bells, the quiet courts, the green lawns, the flurry of gowns, and the hurrying to lectures through the dusk and the lamplit streets—all spoke to him in a voice that he recognized and loved. Tristram Walkinshaw. He had not left him behind. He was here. Everywhere. This was his friend's spiritual home: his dream—long spoken of at Ellenhead—now proved, to Stephen's astonishment, to be wonderfully true. Here, in truth, was a city consecrated to high learning and peace. And it was here, in this unworldly place, that the good man's hopes for him were to be fulfilled. He was to be a scholar. Win prizes. Find self-regard. Fired by such kindly hopes, he flung himself headlong at the themes and exercises set him by his tutors. He rose before dawn to study Euclid. He read Pindar. Wrote Greek verses. Worked furiously to acquit himself well at the Latin declamations.

And then, slowly, his doubts crept in.

What was the point of these studies? Could one put the world to rights by haranguing it in a dead tongue? Discouraged, he began looking at Oxford more critically. Vice-chancellor, proctors, beadles, scarlet gowns, crimson hoods, gold tassels—its medieval mummery suddenly maddened him. The place was a cheat, after all. A mere breeding ground for privilege and sloth.

At the end of a month, he tore up his Latin prose in a rage and made spills with it to light his first pipe.

"Thought it would not last!" laughed a voice through his open door.

And John Taverner, gentleman-commoner, invited himself in.

"You northern barbarians descend on us like a scourge, work like mad dogs for a few weeks, and then . . ."

"Yes? And then *what?*" Stephen shot at him, both angry at the intrusion and perplexed for an answer.

His visitor settled himself in his other chair.

"Then, you find that you're no better off than when you were schoolboys. The same grind. The same authors. The same pedantic trash!"

Stephen grinned. He had not expected this soft-spoken southerner to hit the nail on the head with such force.

"And the grief of it is that there's a world of new ideas— *modern* ideas waiting for us to explore! Montesquieu! Voltaire! Rousseau! The Encyclopedists!"

Stephen tried not to look blank. Montesquieu was not even a name to him.

"And Locke and Adam Smith and Hume . . . and Tom Paine's *Common Sense* . . . and Thomas Jefferson . . ."

Stephen's face lit up.

"The Declaration of Independence!" he exclaimed.

John Taverner slapped his own knee in a gesture of mock congratulation. So news of the American War of Independence had actually reached him in his northern bog, he laughed.

This was absurd! The Americans had won the war six years before. Stephen himself had been so passionately devoted to their cause that at the age of twelve he had dragged the ten-year-old Catherine up to the top of Skelcrag and bawled out Jefferson's mighty words to her, in defiance of the narrow Camberstock valley and the bigoted home out of which they had climbed.

"That's the voice of *free* men!" he had told her.

She had looked puzzled.

"Uncle Fletcher says they're rebels," she had replied with childish doubt.

"I don't live in a bog," Stephen told his new friend, with some spirit. "And I'm neither a fool nor a miserable Tory. I can recite every sentence of that Declaration off to you—pat."

John Taverner suddenly jumped to his feet, his face alive with interest, and clapped him on the shoulder.

"Then, you must join us!" he exclaimed excitedly.

"Join whom?"

"Our debating club. It's political. We read papers. Tear the Government to pieces—that sort of thing."

"Where does the club meet?"

"In Balliol. In Evan Powell's rooms—every Friday night. But, Parkin, not a word to your tutors. It's a secret affair."

Four months later, Catherine made a passionate appeal to her elders.

"But you *must* let him come home," she cried, flushing crimson with distress. "You . . . you can't go on being so cruel."

"Be quiet, child," snapped Uncle Fletcher. "It is not *we* who are to blame. It is solely your brother."

"But what has he *done?*"

"Read this," he replied curtly, tossing over the letter which had brought down this latest wrath on Stephen's head. "Read this. And judge for yourself."

She picked up the letter and read:

St. John's College, Oxford
4th May 1789

Dear Birkett,

First, let me hasten to congratulate Mrs. Birkett and yourself upon the birth of a son. This is an unlooked-for felicity, indeed. I trust that your wife has now left her sickbed and that the child is thriving better than at first.

Now, concerning your nephew, Stephen Parkin. As you bade, I have made inquiries of my good friend, Dr. Bannister, of the same college and regret to inform you that neither his tutors nor the University authorities speak well of the young man. At first, he showed promise of being a clever student and attended his college exercises with zeal; but he has since slackened in his duties and now consorts with a disaffected youth called Taverner, together with whom he has published a notoriously disloyal pamphlet entitled: *Whither Tends This Present Tyranny?* The proctors have confiscated this piece of trash and have threatened its authors with rustication upon a second offense. I must also report that both youths have

been fined frequently for failing to attend their college chapel and
that . . .

Catherine threw away the letter in fury.

"It is not fair!" she cried. "You have set spies on him!"

"Catherine!" gasped Aunt Biddy in horror.

"But it is true!" she hurled at them tearfully from the door.
"You . . . you have no right to set that old man spying on what
Stephen does."

She fled to her room, bitterly angry with her uncle. A father
would have forgiven his son that silly pamphlet, she thought.
But not an uncle! Not an uncle like Uncle Fletcher. Instead, he
had banished Stephen from Town End. She would not see him
again for months and months. And what was to happen to him?
How was Stephen to live—with no money—through the sixteen
weeks of the long vacation?

The answer was vouchsafed her at supper that night.

"Catherine," said Uncle Fletcher coldly. "I expect an apology
for your unjust charge against me. As for your brother, I have
written this morning to our cousin, the Reverend Samuel Crook-
endon, vicar of Toft Lofting in the county of Norfolk, asking
him if he will give lodging and employment to him for the
summer. I do not doubt but that Stephen can assist him on the
glebe farm or in his parish or in starting his small cousins in their
Latin. It matters not, so long as he is out of harm's way. But I
insist again that he shall not be received in this house until he
becomes a more loyal subject to his king and knows how to
conduct himself more properly before the world."

Catherine bowed her head.

"You may see from this," he continued, "that I am concerned
for your brother's health and good name and that I am neither
cruel nor unfair."

She made her apology as contritely as she could—though she
could not help wondering why it was all right for Stephen to be
Stephen in Norfolk but not in Westmorland, until she remembered that the Duke of Ullswater was to take up his summer

residence at the castle in a week's time, and realized that her uncle must fear for his own good name.

But her distress was not yet over for the day.

"That's good, missy," said Uncle Matthew, settling down eagerly to his pork and beans. In his boorish way, he was trying to be kind. "There, see, Fletcher, there's *one* o' t' sister's brood knows how to make amends."

One? What had Josh ever done that he needed to make amends? Stung anew—this time for Josh—she rushed into battle again.

"Josh!" she burst out angrily. "He's done *all* that you've wanted him to do!"

She felt as though the tears might spill out of her eyes.

Josh had come home in April from his terrible first voyage with his hands torn and bleeding from hauling on the frozen sheets. But—far worse—he had returned impenetrably shut up inside himself: a grim, sad boy, whom neither Martha nor herself had been able to get to speak about his life at sea.

"Oh, aye, Joshua," said Uncle Matthew carelessly, stuffing his mouth with food.

"He's got himself into the East India Company's navy," she flared, and then nearly broke down—for not even Captain Fulford's letter to Uncle Parkin saying that he had acquitted himself well had been able to coax Josh out of his despair.

"He's off your hands," she rounded on them all.

"Catherine!" rasped Uncle Fletcher.

"Fletcher, Fletcher," said Aunt Biddy, clutching at his sleeve. "She is tired. She is overspent. The child . . . the child cried all last night . . . and . . . the night before."

It was true. And the sick baby slept in Catherine's room.

"That must be your excuse then, niece," came the cutting reply.

Sick at heart, Catherine escaped to her room again, sat down on her bed, and gazed wretchedly through the spring dusk at the sleeping infant in the cradle below her.

"Poor child," she thought, noting the worried look of its pinched-up mouth. "Will they love you any better than they love

their nephews? Or is there always this bitter war between one
generation and the next?

Thank heavens there was still Martha!

She and Martha had now left school forever; and Martha had
returned from the school boardinghouse at Camberstock to her
father's farm in Garthdale, in Yorkshire. Yet, though separated
by the Pennines, they were still almost as one, for they wrote to
each other daily.

"I am liking my new mother better than I thought," Martha
had written the day before.

"I am hating my uncles worse than ever," she was about to
scribble back.

Thank goodness Martha was coming to stay in Camberstock
for a whole month—at the end of June!

The clash with so much authority cast a damp on the Trinity
Term, not so much because Stephen was averse to such clashes,
but because Uncle Fletcher in his letter of remonstration had
reminded him roundly of his duties towards Catherine.

"You have been granted by us, your guardians, sir, the greater
part of your brother's and sister's small inheritance with the
express purpose that you should work hard at the University,
obtain a good degree, and take holy orders—and thus be in a
position to support your sister and give her a home. And what
have you done instead? Behaved disgracefully towards your king
and country—and squandered your sister's hopes!"

With mounting gloom, Stephen thought of Catherine, gazed
at his duties, and saw that he was trapped.

"They want me to become a *parson!*" he groaned to John
Taverner, tossing the letter aside and staring glumly at his row
of Latin texts. "I've got a sister to support."

"It's the same with me," grimaced his friend, who had just
crumpled up a parental letter and chucked it out into The High.
"They want me to become a lawyer, forsooth! And administer
their devilish laws for the rest of my life!"

They left Stephen's rooms and proceeded in despair to Addison's Walk.

"I know!" exclaimed Stephen excitedly after much pacing, an idea suddenly springing into his mind as fully equipped as Jason's armed men. "We'll leave them their blasted money and emigrate to America! That's what we'll do! I've been rereading More's *Utopia*. We'll take ten members of the Debating Club with us and found an ideal state!"

"Parkin, you're *mad!*" came the cutting reply.

"No, I'm not. What do we hate so much here in England? Unequal laws; the unequal division of land, money, and education. The snobbery; the toadyism. The idiotic king. Well, in *my* state—when we've been granted our tract of virgin land—we'll have laws agreed upon by ourselves. We'll each work five hours a day and share the result. We'll spend the rest of the time reading, talking, writing books! It will be marvelous, Taverner!"

"Don't be a fool. Who'd cook for us . . . milk the cows?"

"Why, we'd take women with us to do that. . . . Marry them! It's simple."

His friend laughed nervously.

"I don't know any sort of woman like that."

"Well, *I* do," he replied.

The memory of a girl in a muslin dress bandaging up his head by the light of bursting rockets had suddenly come into his head.

"But, Parkin, I don't *want* to dig and delve—like a sweaty farmer."

Stephen looked at him in disappointment.

"You don't?"

"Of course I don't. Look at my hands."

Stephen looked.

They were exquisitely gentlemanly—and quite unused to dirt.

"Besides," he continued, now thoroughly roused from his gloom. "We can't leave Europe *now*. Not now, when such tremendous things are about to happen in France.

France was bankrupt—its unwieldy and inefficient administration everywhere dishonored. And, after one hundred and seventy-five years of despotic rule, the monarchy had at last been compelled to summon the States-General to Versailles to advise it on the government of the country. The noblemen, the clergy, and the elected members of the middle classes were, at this very moment, sitting in debate.

"Bah!" exclaimed Stephen in disgust. "They'll settle for a constitutional monarchy—and then, where will they be? Their king is even more wedded to his feudal power than our own. They'll be little better off. Despotism will have but changed its name."

But his friend would not agree. The summoning of the States-General, he held, was like a great crack in a dam wall.

"Parkin," he cried. "I can't wait to see what will happen in France when the water seeps through! The flood will come in with a roar. It will sweep away everything before it—injustice, privilege, every stinking remnant of feudal decay!"

They must stay on here in Oxford, he urged. Do enough of the prescribed reading to keep their tutors quiet and hold themselves in readiness for the mighty events about to take place on the other side of the Channel. He would tell their fellow members of the Debating Club as much, he said.

It seemed a tame way to show one's revolutionary ardor, Stephen grumbled.

Others of his contemporaraies must have thought so, too, for a month later, when the States-General declared itself to be "The National Assembly," a great rumpus broke out in Stephen's sleepy sink of sloth.

Oxford is not entirely a city of dreaming towers and spires. It possesses one huge dome: the dome of the Radcliffe Physic Library, sitting on its base like a gigantic, solemn stone egg.

Hearing shouts of laughter and also of anger coming from the Radcliffe Square, the two friends ran out of their college to find out what was up.

"Great Heaven!" exclaimed John Taverner, gaping at the dome.

Stephen's eyes followed his friend's. Painted round the great egg in letters three feet high was the famous slogan of France's hopes: LIBERTY, EQUALITY, FRATERNITY.

"Did *you* do it?" hissed his friend in his ear.

"No," shouted Stephen in delight. "But, by God, I wish I had!"

Martha began her visit at Town End later than had originally been planned—on Saturday, the eleventh of July.

Three days later, on Tuesday, the fourteenth of July, a letter arrived for Catherine from Stephen in Norfolk. Uncle Fletcher, who had brought the mail with him from Camberstock, handed her the letter and watched her from the other side of the kitchen hearth as she broke the wafer and read its single sheet.

> The Vicarage,
> Toft Lofting,
> By Norwich.

Dear Catherine,

    I want no prying eyes, so burn this letter as soon as you have read it. Tomorrow, I leave this tedious household for Lincoln, where I shall join an Oxford friend in a walking tour to the North. Expect me in Westmorland in ten days' time. I shall send you down word from the hills as to where we may meet. I have told Cousin Samuel that my tutors have summoned me back to Oxford. Tell the uncles what lie you please.

> Your loving brother,
> Stephen.

"What does he say?" asked Uncle Fletcher impatiently.

She crumpled up the letter into a ball and threw it in the fire.

"He is well," she said vaguely, her cheeks beginning to burn.

"Well?" he shot at her. "Of course he is well. Why should your brother *not* be well?"

"I mean . . . I mean," she stammered, trying to gain time, "that he is happy at Cousin Samuel's . . . very happy."

"*Happy?* What nonsense is this?"

"He means, missy," interrupted Uncle Matthew, laughing, "why did you burn t' letter?"

"It was of no importance," she managed to say carelessly with a shrug of her shoulders. "Except that he has to leave."

"Leave?" snapped Uncle Fletcher. "Leave Toft Lofting? But he has not my permission to leave!"

His tutors had summoned Stephen back to Oxford, she told him as she watched the ball of paper slowly crumble into ash.

Later, when she was alone with Martha, she told her friend the true contents of the letter, and was startled beyond measure to find how angry they made her.

"Catherine!" she exclaimed sternly. "It is *wrong* of Stephen—very wrong—for him to force you into telling lies for him."

"Knowing Uncle Fletcher," she replied hotly, "what else could he do?"

"*Obey* him—for a change. Your uncle is harsh with him, but not entirely unjust."

Catherine bit back an angry retort. She was heartsick, and could not bear to quarrel with her only friend.

"Stephen is behaving very badly," Martha continued without mercy. "He is thoughtless and willful. He has *your* future at stake—and he knows it!"

It was true. Catherine could not deny it. The humiliation of it brought the tears to her eyes.

Ten days later, peace restored between them, the two girls were waiting far up in Camberdale Glen at the appointed meeting place, in a valley so remote from human habitation that it was frequented only by wild ponies and red deer. In the midday stillness, not a bird sang; not a creature moved. Even the mountain streams seemed half asleep.

"They are late," murmured Martha. "It is nearly one o'clock."

"They will come," said Catherine, herself feeling drowsy in the summer heat. "It is the place Stephen said."

She felt infinitely content to sit there, waiting for her brother, knowing that—however selfish and unloving he might appear to others—he was coming all this way to be with her for an hour.

At that moment, a spatter of small stones fell upon the flat rock on which they were sitting, and turning round, they saw two figures high up the steep escarpment immediately above them. Now they disappeared, hidden for a space by an outcrop of rock, but their voices came down to them, thin and high in the still air.

"It's Stephen!" exclaimed Catherine, jumping up. "He's excited about something."

"And so's his friend," said Martha, listening to the quick interchange of men's voices.

Then, suddenly, they came into view much lower down the hill, scarcely fifty feet above them, and the small stones they dislodged on the mountain track came bouncing down towards them.

Stephen caught sight of them at last, whereupon the joy of the news that he had to bring them, burst out of him like a cannonball.

"Catherine!" he shouted with a mighty shout, hurtling down the precipitous slope towards her. "It's *begun!* It's *begun!*"

"What's begun?" she asked laughing, as he missed his footing and came slithering down the last six yards on his seat.

"The Revolution!" he shouted triumphantly, coming to rest at her feet.

"What revolution?" asked both the girls.

"The people of Paris . . ." shouted his friend, careering down the slope in his wake. "The people of Paris . . . have risen at last!"

"The Bastille has fallen!" Stephen exclaimed.

He was so drunk with the joy of it that he scrambled to his feet and flung his arms round his sister.

"Goodness!" she murmured, happy and foolish. "The Bastille? Whatever's that?"

"The Bastille?" he barked, bitterly disappointed at her ignorance and holding her now at arm's length. "Haven't you heard of the Bastille?"

She shook her head.

"It's a prison," explained John Taverner. "The people have killed the governor and stuck his head on a pike."

"Oh, how dreadful!" gasped Martha.

"It was his own fault," Stephen frowned at the girl. "They asked him to surrender the fortress in the name of the nation . . . and he fired on them. *Fired* on them! Think of that!"

"You see, it's like this . . ." explained his fellow undergraduate, taking up the tale and describing the misery of the French peasants and the cruelty of their landlords, the weakness of the king and the folly of the queen, and the terrible inefficiency of the Government.

"And on top of it all," continued Stephen, "the harvest has failed. The people are starving."

"Then, why are you so pleased?"

It was Martha, looking puzzled and unhappy.

He looked at her piercingly—this girl that he would have taken with him to found his American Utopia, seeing her properly for the first time. She was handsome and sensible—and strong.

Just the girl!

"Because it is the end of tyranny," he answered her candidly.

Now that the people of Paris had shown their power, went on John Taverner, addressing the two girls as though they were members of his Debating Club, the king could no longer govern without them. . . . The long centuries of despotism were at an end. And, it was not only in Paris that Frenchmen were throwing off their chains. Every big city was rumbling with discontent. The fall of the Bastille had shown them the way. . . . True liberty was within the nation's grasp.

His soft, southern voice purled on, interrupted every now and then by Stephen's northern burr.

"Catherine!" her brother shouted. "You're not listening!"

She came back to them all, there in the quiet valley, to find Martha looking greatly upset.

"No. No. What were you saying?"

"Taverner and I are going to see it for ourselves."

"See what?"

"The Revolution!"

"The Revolution?" she asked blankly. "You mean you're . . . you're going to France?"

"Yes."

"But what will Uncle Fletcher say?" she blurted out.

" 'Uncle Fletcher.' 'Uncle Fletcher,' " he mocked her. "Who the devil cares what Uncle Fletcher says? We are not children."

"But . . . but Oxford?"

"We'll be back by the Michaelmas Term," Stephen's friend assured her.

"But . . . you've no money."

They were going to walk through northern France. They would not need much, the stranger continued.

"I'll sell Father's gold watch and his snuffbox and his chain," put in Stephen.

"No. No, you mustn't," she burst out, appalled that he should squander these precious keepsakes on such a spree.

"Why not? They're mine."

"But . . . but it's all we've got left of Father!"

"Father's dead."

"Stephen!"

"Well, it's the future that matters, not the past," he replied, turning his head away to avoid Martha's steady gaze.

"And the future lies in France, Miss Parkin."

"What's the good of *you* going to France?" she rounded angrily on her brother. "You don't even speak French—at least, not so that any Frenchman could understand you!"

"I do," said his friend. "We'll get along."

With a fresh spurt of anger, she turned again to Stephen.

"And what am I to say to them at Town End?" she asked bitterly. "What lie must I tell now?"

He shrugged his shoulders.

"What you like."

"No. It is not fair!" exclaimed Martha, surprisingly loud. "Catherine must tell no more lies on your account. You must tell your own."

He looked at her again, then. Handsome and strong, she was —and unexpectedly stern. He had not known before that a girl could have such strength.

"They do not know that you are meeting us here?" he asked Catherine more gently.

She shook her head.

"Then they need not know about our going to France," he said, beginning to smile.

"But what about *me?*" she cried in anguish. He was abandoning her yet again. "Am *I* not to know where you are or how you fare?"

"I'll get word to you. I'll write."

"No," said Martha firmly.

They all looked at her in surprise.

"You must not write to Catherine at Town End."

"Why not?"

Martha described the embarrassment caused by his last letter.

"It's true," added Catherine. "I think if Uncle Fletcher were pushed to it, he would open your letters to me and read them himself. He might even destroy them before letting me see them."

"Then what's to be done?" he asked.

"Easy," said John Taverner. "Write to Miss Parkin's friend, instead. Miss Penrose can pass on our news with no fear of interception."

Stephen glanced at their stern go-between, amused—and yet oddly excited to hear her reply.

"I don't like it," she said after a long pause. "But for Catherine's sake, you may write to me at Garthdale. I will do as you ask."

Half an hour later, the girls watched them climb up the mountain path.

Then, they stooped down and gathered together the remains of their picnic.

"I don't like his friend," said Martha, trying to give Catherine some comfort. "He leads your brother astray."

Catherine shook her head. She doubted that. She knew Stephen far better than did Martha.

4

France

Putting Catherine and her stern-eyed friend—and the white cliffs of Dover—behind him, Stephen turned his face gaily towards France. It was a pity that there was a thick blanket of mist.

And then the packet boat suddenly sailed out of it.

"Look!" exclaimed Taverner, clutching his arm and pointing southward. "There it is! That's the coast!"

"That bank?"

His friend nodded.

"It looks very flat!"

What had he expected? White cliffs? Another fortressed isle?

For the five long hours of the crossing, he could not tear himself away from the rail. The gray bank slowly deepened and widened till it stretched as far as the eye could see. Now, it colored faintly. Now, he could see sand dunes and greensward and a gray village, its sharp-roofed houses clustered in a low hollow. He took a deep breath. They were coming to a countryside swept clean of hedges and trees and hills, a land lying clear-cut and harsh under the pouring light.

With a sudden flapping of sails and tipping of the deck, the packet swung on the starboard tack, and he saw three fishing boats quite close below them. He grinned at the fishermen's upturned faces—and shouted them a greeting.

"They won't understand *that!*" laughed his companion. "Perhaps they'll understand *this.*"

First he waved; then he clenched both hands above his head in an unmistakable gesture of congratulations and accord. The nut-brown faces in the nearest boat broke into smiles. The fishermen pulled off their caps and waved back.

"*Les Anglais,*" one of them shouted.

Then they laughed.

Every moment, the land beyond the fishing boats was growing brighter and more sharply distinct. They could see the ware-houses and the low buildings of a meager port.

Five minutes later, the quays of Calais unfolded from the shore to welcome them in. The packet boat glided noiselessly into the harbor.

"Well?" asked Taverner, a smile playing about his lips.

Stephen gazed spellbound at his first French town and at the motley crowd awaiting their berthing.

They were standing now on the quayside, Taverner with his valise, himself carrying his spare coat and breeches tied up in a

red-spotted handkerchief, deafened by the shouts and laughter and the gabble of strange speech, his nose pricking to the smells of tar, tallow, garlic, and sweat.

"Welcome, citizens," cried a porter, grasping them warmly by the hand. "Welcome to France!"

"Welcome, citizen!" they grinned back.

They were off now, their porter carrying their modest luggage on his shoulders and shouting *"Les Anglais! Les Anglais!"* as he barged his way through the throng.

"We must get our passports for Paris," Taverner shouted over the babel.

"But we're not going to *Paris!*" he shouted back.

"Yes we are—now that we're here."

As the cabriolet swung out of Calais and took the road to Boulogne, Stephen was beside himself with vexation.

"We agreed to go on a *walking* tour," he protested angrily.

He did not want to go to Paris. He knew nothing about great cities. Besides, he had not the money. His father's trinkets had been worth very little.

"Believe me," explained John Taverner cheerfully. "There'll be nothing worth seeing in this waste. It's in Paris that they're fighting for freedom."

"Why did you deceive me?"

His companion shrugged his shoulders and laughed.

"It was the best way to persuade you to come."

Stephen stared out at the dunes and the yellow-horned poppies in raging self-contempt. He had let himself be duped—cheated by this specious, gentlemanly rogue. And the worst of it was that there was no way out of the mess. With little money and less French, he was handcuffed to him for the next three weeks.

After Boulogne, they headed south and drove across a vast plain where every evidence of man seemed dwarfed and rendered pitiful by the immensity of the sky. With his countryman's eyes, he gazed wretchedly at the ruined barns, the poor hovels, and the miserably neglected farms. Here was desolation, indeed—and a terrible indictment of the landlords. And what the indifference of the landowners had begun, the fearful storms of the past weeks had completed. The wheat and barley were rotting where they grew. Great tracts of land lay waterlogged and glistening in the sun. The few people that he saw about in the fields moved as slowly as their cows.

John Taverner was studying a street map of Paris. They had not spoken for miles.

"Are they everywhere as wretched?" he asked suddenly.

His companion looked up.

"Do you mean the peasants?" he asked carelessly. "Why, yes. They have always and everywhere been wretched. The poor dolts pay most of the country's taxes."

He returned to his map.

Soon afterwards, they passed a woman in rags, forking dung into a cart. She looked up at them, and Stephen saw that her face was old and hollow—like a skull's. Then, he saw the shape of her body and gasped. She was pregnant.

He snatched the map out of Taverner's hands.

"*Tell* me about the French peasants," he demanded fiercely.

Taverner looked up in surprise; then shrugged his shoulders and smiled.

"Very well," he said. "The French peasant pays heavy taxes to his Government, tithes to his greedy Church, and—in times of war—hands over his sons and his cattle to the military. If the harvest is good, he may just survive. If it fails, he starves. That's all there is to say about him. 'Jacques Bonhomme' is a bearer of burdens. A mule. A jackass. If he's pressed too hard, he'll kick out with his hoof. He's too stupid and downtrodden to do much else."

"And is the Revolution not for him, also?" Stephen asked indignantly.

"Yes, I suppose, in time. When the people of Paris have shown him the way."

And he took back his map.

An hour later, with the same flatness and the same desolation to be seen whichever way one turned, Stephen at last made up his mind.

"I'm leaving you," he told his companion. "Tell the driver to put me down at the next crossroads."

"*Leaving* me? What do you mean?"

"I'm not going to Paris."

"You're joking."

He shook his head and scowled out eastward where the clouds were massing low in the sky.

"You're going back to England?"

"No. I'm going out there," he said savagely, jabbing his thumb in the direction of the coming storm.

"Into *that*? Parkin, you're mad!"

The wet fields of rotting crops stretched unbroken to the horizon.

"What will you find there? Nothing. Brutes—living like brutes. How will you live? How will you make yourself understood?"

He was not a fool, he replied. One countryman could converse with another countryman without the use of words.

The cabriolet was slowing to a halt.

John Taverner's voice rose an octave in panic.

"Come with me to Paris," he begged, now nearly desperate for his company. "It's Paris that you ought to see. It's the heart of France. The brains of France. The soul of France."

As Stephen picked up his red-spotted bundle, he grinned at him hugely. He had paid him back for his deception.

"Well, I'm for its rump," he said, as he climbed down onto the road.

"What if something happens to you?" Taverner shouted after him.

"Nothing will," he tossed back.

"I shan't be able to face your sister."

He turned round and laughed at him.

"Then, *don't!*"

He sat out the storm in a tumbledown shed which he found just over the brow of the long slope he had climbed from the Paris road. The shed smelled of pig. A sow in farrow must have used it last.

He was alone now. Alone as he had never been before. And he found the experience singularly uninspiring. Catherine. Martha. Oxford. England. His dishonest friend. He had pushed them all behind him in order to sit here in a French pigsty! In front of him, the whole landscape was blotted out by the sheeting rain, while outside, huge puddles were forming in the stubble. Behind him, the storm had found a weakness in the thatch; drops of water were bouncing down on the brim of his hat. Damn the rain! One could not set fire to the world in weather like this. One could hardly save one's own small flame from a dousing.

He pulled up his coat collar, buried his hands in his pockets, and thought about . . . Calais.

Then, he smiled.

"Welcome, citizen! Welcome to France!"

A sweaty porter had grasped his hand!

Half an hour later, the rain blew off to the west, the sky lightened, and the country below put on color and distinctness.

He stood up and stared.

At his feet lay a valley green with orchards and small patches of alfalfa and beans; over the tops of the orchard trees he could see the roofs of a small village, a church spire, and a rocklike building—a *château* perhaps—dominating the quiet scene from a low height. There was a small river somewhere and a weir, for he could hear the splash of water. Beyond the village stretched a ridge of hills covered with trees.

He sighed with relief. He had come to the end of the pitiless plain. He shook the water out of his hat, picked up his bundle, and strode down the hill.

Yet, as he drew nearer, the bright vision put on rags. Here, too, was desolation. He could not understand it at first. The wheat crops had been ravaged by the storms; they were also alive with

pheasants and partridges, strutting unmolested and eating up such of the harvest as still remained.

The patches of beans and alfalfa were trampled down as though by wild beasts. And when he descended to the orchards, he saw that the trunks of the apple trees were stripped of their bark. Then, it came to him. That was it. The whole valley was infested with deer. His eye caught the great *château* frowning down upon the vale. And he understood. He ground his teeth. A French "Duke of Ullswater" had dominion here. These poor men's fields were his hunting preserve.

It was evening.

As he approached the first houses of the village, he saw that the sky was darkening over the wooded hills. Back home, it would have been the hour for the first blue wood smoke to come curling up out of the cottage chimneys; for children to leave their play; for men to trek homeward behind their cows. Here, in this French valley, there was silence. He was suddenly struck by the ominous hush. Not only were there no villagers—there were no cattle; no goats; no cocks; no hens. There was not a living creature to be seen—save the game in the crops and a flock of starlings flying overhead.

He entered the paltry street and stared uneasily at the shuttered windows of the hovels. Had there been a plague here? Were the people all dead? Yet, as he walked cautiously, looking this way and that, down the middle of the puddled way, he smelled garbage—but not death. His heart thumped inside him. He was afraid. There was no doubt of it. He, who could have stared a seen terror out of countenance, was frightened by the lurking menace of this place. He crossed the deserted square and came to the church and stared up questioningly at the starved Christ in the crucifix outside. No answer there. No answer, yet, from the grim fortress of the *château* across the way. Near to panic, he wished that he were back home with Catherine and her friend —or fooling about Oxford with that ass Taverner. Not here. Alone. In this terrible hush.

Fearful of what horror might lie behind him, he began walk-

ing quickly down the far end of the street—and out of the place.

And then—as he was passing the last wretched hovel—he heard it!

A child's whimper! Quickly smothered!

He stopped in surprise and listened, noting the single window nailed up with an old board. Then, he walked closer and stood under the eaves, and heard the faint clucking of hens within. He stood on the threshold, irresolute. He was hungry. He stood perfectly still, holding his breath, and with the sharp instinct of a night poacher became aware that someone was standing on the far side of the barred door, listening too.

Gripping his bundle of clothes firmly in his left hand, he rapped loudly with the knuckles of his right.

After a full half minute, the door opened a few inches and a pair of wild eyes set in a haggard face peered out at him.

Seeing his English hat, the woman let out a howling shriek and slammed the door in his face.

"Welcome to France!" he thought bitterly, as he sat up in an apple tree in the first orchard that he had come to, and stared back in the dying light at the haunted village through which he had come.

What had frightened the peasants so much? Why had they barricaded themselves in their hovels? Did they fear plague? Bandits? The Duke? Witchcraft? Whatever it was, it had cost him a sorry night. He was cold and hungry—and he had nothing to eat but the few mildewed apples still hanging on the trees. He was uncomfortable, too. It was too wet to lie on the grass.

Damn this whole stupid enterprise. What a fool he had been!

Then—in the middle of his self-disgust—he pricked up his ears. The clopping of hoofs? Horsemen were approaching from a long way off, riding fast. As he listened to their thudding, he was swept with relief. The nightmare was over. He was back in the known world of hurry and noise and rider and mount. He stood up in his tree and eagerly scanned the hills for their coming. But it was too dark. It was almost night. He listened, instead; listened carefully to the drumming tattoo of the hoofbeats. Two horsemen—three—not more—were galloping up the long slope from the Paris road which he had climbed himself not four hours before. And now, with the sudden thundering of their hoofs, he knew that they were over the brow. They were galloping headlong down into the valley.

Highwaymen? Bandits? Was their coming what the peasants had feared? Was he about to witness murder and arson and looting?

And yet—only two or three? Could a village not protect itself against so few?

He jumped down from his tree and, under cover of the deepening dusk, walked back towards the first hovel, listening intently to the oncoming riders.

They had entered the far end of the street now and were shouting a wild halloo. Not savage. Joyful. They were shouting the same words over and over again, seeming to tell the peasants shut up in their huts of some wonderful deliverance, some cause for rejoicing.

He had come to the church, now, and stood in the darkness of the porch, watching.

Still they shouted their good news—and went on shouting it as they clattered into the square.

He caught it at last.

"The Duke!" they were shouting. "The Duke has fled to Holland!"

The peasants caught it, too. Out of the hovels crept three figures, four, five—cautious householders making certain that they were not tricked. Then, recognizing the horsemen dismounting before the barred gate of the *château,* they let out a howl of savage joy. The dead village awoke on the instant. In front of his astonished eyes, the square was suddenly thronged with yelling men and women, screeching children, barking dogs, goats, cows, hens.

Every living creature seemed to have its face turned towards the *château* gate. Every peasant raised his arm and shook his fist at the grim fortress.

Stephen slipped out of the church porch and joined the throng. The three riders were hammering on the locked postern, demanding admittance. In the silence that followed, he saw the faces of the angry crowd, luridly lit up by the light of a flaring torch; they were hollow-eyed, cadaverous—like that of the woman who had been forking dung.

At no answer from within, the peasants' fury burst out afresh, and Stephen felt himself pushed along with the crowd towards the barred gate.

The fools! he thought, staring ahead of him at the stout oaken beams. They would have to scale the walls and unlock those gates from inside.

As if in answer to his thought, one of the young horsemen clambered up on the stone coping of the moat bridge, sprang onto a narrow ledge of the castle wall some ten feet above the water, and began climbing up the rough face of the crumbling stonework. Stephen watched him. The man was in too much of a hurry. He knew nothing about climbing. About twenty feet up, he missed his footing and, with a disappearing yell, fell into the moat.

Without a moment's reflection, Stephen jumped up on the coping of the bridge in the man's place. He would show them. He would show these French idiots how a man should climb a rock face. He leaped sideways onto the projection over the water and then strained his eyes through the darkness at the crannies and fissures between the undressed blocks of stone above his head. Very slowly, by thought-out foothold and careful handgrip, he climbed thirty feet up the castle wall. Then he had to straddle, spread-eagled, to the next foothold, four feet to his left. Then up, up to a ledge, half overgrown with rock cress, where some bird had built its nest. Looking down for a moment in a pause to gain breath, he saw a southern face grinning up at him from twelve feet below. He grinned back. At least one of the young riders had followed his lead. Farther down still, he saw the people of the village thronged on the moat bridge with upturned faces, streaked red by the torchlight, watching him in astonished silence.

He turned back to the wall face and looked upward for his next handgrip. His heart was throbbing with excitement.

Without thought at what he was doing, he had suddenly become a part of France's Revolution. And as he stood, at length, triumphant and panting on the parapet, hearing the wild yells of the peasants below and looking down for the young rider to come up to him, he felt that he had thrown in his lot with these people—for life.

Once his French companion was up at his side, they turned to a flat, inner part of the roof flanked by dormer windows. They smashed the nearest casement and climbed into an attic. Once out of the attic, they clattered round and round down a spiral staircase inside a corner turret, to the inner courtyard of the *château*. At the foot of the staircase, they flung aside an old retainer who tried to bar their way, ran to the gatehouse, pinioned the porter, snatched off his belt of keys, and finally unbolted and unlocked the stout oaken gate.

In through the gap swept the howling tide.

Unprepared for its force, Stephen found himself pressed flat against the gatehouse wall, a high-pitched, maniacal baying deafening his ears. Then he was hurled inwards—a stick thrown into a torrent—and he was battling among rags and sweat and thrusting legs. His ankle was shot with pain. He was under their clogs, their naked feet.

He came to himself later, lying flat on his back, staring up at the stars.

"My God! Wherever am I?" he muttered aloud.

His head throbbed. He felt bruised in every limb.

Out of the darkness came the answer:

"In the courtyard, *mon ami,* of the *château* of the Duke of St. Gilles."

There was a hint of laughter in the old man's voice.

Château? St. Gilles? That was it! He was in France!

He sat up painfully and stared through the darkness at the grizzled old man sitting on the cobbles at his side. He looked as battered as himself. He had a wooden leg.

"What's happening?"

There was something confusing about the old man—but he felt so shaken that he could not think what. Besides, wild shouts of buried laughter were coming up from under their feet.

"My neighbors!" laughed the old fellow. "They are in the Duke's cellars. They are drinking his wine."

That was it! Now he knew what was wrong with him!

"You're speaking *English!*" he burst out, his head clearing a little in his surprise.

"It is so," nodded the old cripple, his eyes gleaming with amusement.

"Who are you?"

"Janvier. Pierre Janvier. An old soldier of France."

"And how come you to speak English?"

Janvier shrugged his shoulders and got awkwardly to his feet.

"Our gallant Montcalm. Your General Wolfe. I was taken prisoner by your army in front of Quebec."

Thirty years ago!

"Come!" he said. "Can you get to your feet?"

Stephen scrambled up—and then cried out with pain.

"Your ankle?"

He nodded. He felt sick with shame. He had come all this way. Done so much. And sprained his stupid ankle!

But there was no time to think of ankles. The quiet courtyard was suddenly made hideous with screams. The women of the village, who had been ransacking the upper chambers, had smashed open one of the mullion windows and were throwing out pillows and mattresses and chamberpots and chairs. Feathers and laughter filled the air.

"Come, my son," shouted the old soldier. "The lame must help the lame."

As they hobbled together towards the open gate, a shot rang out. Then another.

"Mon Dieu!" cried his companion. "They have broken into the armory!"

He hurried Stephen over the bridge and across the square as more shots rang out, and more drunken screams.

"They will be shooting at each other in another few minutes," Janvier cried hoarsely, as he pushed him in front of him into his small cabin.

Three whole days and nights it took for the people of St. Gilles to wreak their vengeance on their feudal lord. Stephen and old Janvier sat on the floor of his hut, listening to their yells. In their drunkenness, they murdered the Duke's butler and his porter and two aged gentlewomen found cowering in the attics. They burned his books. They smashed his gilded mirrors, broke open his chests, emptied his grain store, looted salon and bedchamber, saddlery and coachhouse, and took ladder and chisel and hammer and chipped away his armorial bearings over the gate. In one terrible, headlong carousal, they blotted out his name and drank themselves insensible to the shame he had made them bear.

In the hush of the fourth morning, Stephen's old host got up early and tied on his wooden leg.

"And now," he said, smiling. "I am going out to shoot the deer. When I come back, we—too—shall rejoice!"

A fortnight later, his ankle almost healed, Stephen was carried to the next village on the shoulders of the people of St. Gilles. He was their hero! Their fellow citizen!

"Come back to us, Etienne," said old Janvier, wringing his hand.

He walked slowly back towards the coast in a golden daze. It was the joy that lived with him—not the bloodshed: the joy of passing through one poor village after another that had newly awakened to its freedom. At every wayside shrine, the Virgin Mary smiled down on him with the tricolor ribbon of the Revolution newly pinned to her robe. On the village greens, young and old were dancing *cotillons* under the trees.

The golden age had come again. He was walking here in its dawn.

5

Quartet

But, alas, it was a false dawn!

The golden age had not yet returned either for France or for Stephen himself.

In France, it is true, the National Assembly had published a Declaration of Rights and had given the country a new constitution. Feudalism was dead. But the King remained—as did the foolish Queen. And many of the old abuses, as well.

Once back in Oxford, the two friends soon discovered how unfounded their hopes had been.

"You were right, Parkin," John Taverner remarked wryly. "Great expectations! Much travail! And France has labored and brought forth a mouse! The French have ended up with a constitutional monarchy, after all."

For Stephen, it was a strangely disturbing year. After the burst of excitement at St. Gilles, he was disappointed at the slow pace men took to put the world to rights. But, worse than this, he was at odds with himself—pulled this way and that in his mind—in a way that he did not understand. When he had looked down from the parapet of the *château* upon the villagers of St. Gilles, he had been drunk with exultation. This was his dedication. He had given himself to France—to the world! Yet, afterwards, in the long days of his ankle's mending, lying on Janvier's mud floor and visited hourly by the peasants jabbering their thanks to him in a dialect he could barely understand, he had felt a great hunger for the noble accents of his mother tongue. His host could jest with him in his soldier's argot, but it was Shakespeare that he wanted, and Milton and Pope. He had longed for pure English; for the lovely cadences of his native speech. Later, as he had journeyed back through northern France, rejoicing most truly at the happiness that he saw in the freed hamlets of that ugly plain, he had felt an inexplicable yearning for the mountains of home.

It was no better when he was back at Oxford. He sat down to write his promised letter to Catherine and—addressing it, as agreed, to Miss Penrose—saw her friend's steady eyes watching him as he wrote. What would Martha think of the events at St. Gilles? he wondered. He mended his pen and his memories under the influence of her gaze. He wrote of liberty; not of bloodshed. Of feasting and singing and dancing under the trees; not of the old gentlewomen hacked down in the attics or of the porter's brains spilled out on the cobbles.

And, when he had finished his letter, he flung himself at his Pindar and Euclid, hoping to find peace from his confusion in a fierce intellectual grind.

Peace did not come.

Still banished by his uncles from Catherine and Town End, he took himself off to Ellenhead at the end of term and spent Christmas again with Mr. Walkinshaw.

"This violence," asked his friend, as they walked the frostbound hills. "When will it stop?"

"It won't stop," he replied fiercely. "Not till the last man on earth has been freed from his chains."

"But, my dear Stephen, could one not teach men to loose their neighbors' chains without all this bloodshed and hate?"

He smiled at the unworldly schoolmaster and shook his head.

"The power of the rich is too absolute," he said. "The poor have waited too long for their rights."

Tristram Walkinshaw sighed. And they walked on in silence.

But it was not the silence of peace. Outwardly so certain of what he believed, Stephen was inwardly torn in two. He loved freedom. He believed passionately in the cause of the French

Revolution. He would, if need be, die for that cause. Yet, he was *English*—not French. He belonged not at St. Gilles, nor even in Paris. But here—in these hills.

"You are working harder at Oxford this term?" asked his friend, not unkindly, to change the subject.

He nodded his head.

But for what purpose he was working harder, God only knew!

For Catherine it was a sad year, too.

She felt abandoned. She hated her life at Town End. She watched a cold winter drift into a bleak spring, and the spring, in its turn, fade into a summer of scudding cloud under which the waters of the lake slapped as lusterless as lead. Stephen was banished; and no word came to her from Josh at Calcutta, sweltering in the *Earl of Cape Wrath* far up the River Hooghly. And when, in the middle of June, Aunt Biddy confessed timidly that another baby was to be expected in the household before Christmas, she bowed her head and mourned to see her youth slip by in tending other people's children. When was *she* going to start living life on her own account? When—oh, *when*—was one of her two brothers going to fetch her away?

She was impatient, she knew. She still had Martha. And Stephen seemed to be doing his best. He was behaving himself, at last. If his improvement continued, Uncle Fletcher announced at the beginning of July, then the young man might be allowed back to Camberstock for his winter vacation.

But December! It was five dreary months away!

And then, the glorious thing happened!

One sunny morning a week later, she walked into Camberstock to exchange her novel at the lending library and happened to enter the Clappergate at the very moment that the London coach pulled up outside the *King's Head*.

That's a splendid sight for Camberstock! she thought, as she watched a tall young man leap down from the outside seat and stand with his back to her, demanding his box.

His crimson breeches set the cold, gray street ablaze.

And then, her heart suddenly turned over inside her. The young man had turned his head. It was Josh!

"Josh!" she cried, running towards him. Then, she suddenly stopped in panic. It could not be Josh. She had made a mistake. This man in the gorgeous breeches was huge. He was nearly six feet tall.

The giant turned round.

"Ca-Catherine!" he barked out in delight, grinning all over his face.

It was Josh, indeed. She flung herself into his arms and buried her cheek against his blue uniform coat.

"But where've you dropped from?" she laughed, holding him away from her and proudly taking in the sturdy, sun-browned face, the square shoulders, and the crimson waistcoat to match the incredible breeches.

"The Lo-London coach," he stammered out.

"I thought you were in India."

"B-berthed at Gravesend last week."

Then he turned to the coachman.

"Hurry there with my b-box," he shouted peremptorily.

Goodness! she thought. It was not only his looks that had changed.

"London t-two days ago. Now here. Uncle Parkin's given me ten days. Then b-back to Gravesend. Had t-trouble with her after the C-Cape. She's got to b-be copper-b-bottomed."

She did not understand what he was talking about, but it hardly mattered. He was striding down the Clappergate with his sea chest perched on his shoulder, and she was at his side.

"But why didn't you write?" she asked, running to keep abreast of him.

And then she remembered how much Josh had always hated writing letters.

"Waste of t-time," he replied cheerfully. "I kn-knew you'd be here."

Yes, indeed. Where else would she be? Unless over at Garthdale with Martha.

The same thought must have come to Josh, for he came to a sudden halt.

"Your f-friend?" he asked, blushing under his sunburn.

"Martha?"

"Is she m-married?"

"Martha married? Goodness, no!"

He let out a huge sigh of contentment.

They had come now to St. Kentigern's churchyard, and here Josh suddenly lowered his heavy sea chest and put it down on the low wall which separated the graveyard from the busy street.

"L-look," he said, opening the lid and rummaging under a pile of his East India Company black silk stockings. "L-look. Do you think she'll l-like this?"

And he pulled out a most beautiful Indian silk shawl.

"For *Martha?*" exclaimed Catherine, astonished beyond measure to realize how it must be with her brother.

He mistook the tone of her surprise.

"I've g-got one for you, t-too," he said hurriedly, unearthing yet another beautiful shawl.

"Oh, Josh! They're lovely," she murmured, moved almost to tears not only by the generosity of this stranger of a brother, but also because she remembered the poor booby of a boy who had gone off to sea all those months ago and—seemingly—left his heart behind with her friend.

"They're what l-ladies like?" he asked anxiously.

"Yes. Yes," she assured him. Every lady in Westmorland would envy them both. Shawls were all the rage. Especially Indian shawls. And most especially such lovely shawls as these.

"I'm so g-glad," he stammered in relief. "I've brought back two d-dozen of them."

"*Two dozen!* Whatever for?"

"To-to sell in the London market."

It was his private trade, he explained. He had invested the whole of the fifteen guineas Uncle Matthew had given him in Indian shawls, and with luck he would make a fifty per cent profit.

They were both now sitting on the wall with the spilled-out contents of his chest heaped between them.

"They all do it," he said. "All the officers. And the m-men, too. That's how they get rich."

Not one of them could make a fortune out of his naval pay; it was barely enough to live on. But each rank had a fixed tonnage set aside for one's own private trade. And if one was clever in what one chose to buy and sell, one might well become almost wealthy. Josh grinned happily as he spoke. The chief mate of the *Earl of Spey,* he said, had made his fortune last season by taking out a pack of hounds from England and selling it at a huge profit in Calcutta.

"Uncle P-Parkin says he'll make me f-fourth mate next voyage. And a f-fourth mate g-gets a qu-quarter of a ton for his private t-trade."

Catherine looked across at her brother, her mind in a whirl. Here was a change, indeed.

"So you're a kind of merchant," she observed wonderingly, not at all sure that she liked this change.

Josh made a grimace.

"That's what I'd l-like to be—if I had the m-money to b-buy g-goods."

Out of all reason, she suddenly felt very disappointed in this new Josh.

"I always thought you wanted to be a farmer," she said sadly.

"B-but Catherine, that's—that's what I *do* want to be!"

She looked across at him. There he was—the old Josh—with his mouth hanging open in surprise.

"You d-don't think I *like* the sea, do you? Or—or that d-dreadful heat? Or—or all those thousands of people t-talking a language I c-can't understand?"

She smiled at him. She had been stupid.

As she smiled, a shaft of sunlight poured down from between two scudding clouds and caught the top of Camberstock Hill.

"Th-that's wh-what I want!" exclaimed Josh with fervor, pointing over the rooftops at the sheep grazing on the sunlit slopes. "Th-that's all I've *ever* wanted!"

He did not mind what he bought or sold, he said, or how sharp and mean he became in the process—so long as he could save enough money to buy himself a small hill farm.

"Oh, Josh!" she cried, looking first at the amber hill and then back at her brother's face. "I'm so *happy* that you are back!"

If Josh was no letter writer, the same could not be said of his Uncle Parkin.

As soon as the gallant captain had seen to the unloading of

68 *Quartet*

his cargo and presented his report to the Court of Directors, he
settled himself comfortably in his old London lodgings and
scattered letters abroad with the abandon of a man setting out
on a paper chase. To do him justice, he had eighteen months to
catch up with, not only as a ship's commander, a merchant, and
the uncle to his brother's children, but also as a bachelor who was
uncommonly fond of the ladies.

Requests for new timbers, water casks, cables, and canvas went
fluttering east downriver to the ship's chandlers, while northwards into Yorkshire blew a gale of angry notes about last voyage's putrid hams.

To Catherine, he sent a draft on his bank for thirty guineas.

"Dear Niece," he wrote. "You are a good girl, I hear. But at
eighteen, even virtue needs a pretty dress!"

And to Stephen at Oxford, he scratched a peremptory:

"Your Uncle Fletcher complains you're a damned radical. I'm
sorry to hear it. Keep better company, boy. Learn to trim your
sails, like your younger brother. That's the way to get on!"

Only then—with his duty done—did this gnarled and middle-
aged commander of the *Earl of Cape Wrath* mend his pen and
write a summons to his mistress living on the farther side of
town.

On the evening of Josh's arrival, Catherine hurried back to Camberstock to catch the night mail, two hastily scribbled letters in
her hand.

The first read as follows:

Dear Stephen,
JOSH IS HOME—for 10 days! Uncle Fletcher is away in Scotland
on the D's business. So come *quickly*.
Love, Catherine.

The second letter was to Martha. Josh was home, she wrote.
Uncle Fletcher was in Scotland. So, *please* would she come?

Three days later, Stephen, Martha, Catherine, and Josh were all four together for the first time in their lives.

"Josh!" shouted Stephen, jumping down from the roof of the coach.

"S-Stephen!"

"My God!" he laughed, his eyes level with Josh's happy grin. "What on earth have they fed you on for the last eighteen months?"

"B-biscuit and b-b-bad ham," Josh burst out, laughing in return.

Stephen was delighted to be home with them. He could hardly contain his joy.

"And Catherine . . . and Martha," he cried, sweeping the two girls away from the dismounting passengers, an arm round each of their waists. "And no Uncle Fletcher! Hurray!"

"Shush!" laughed Catherine, trying to cover his mouth up with her hand. "Everyone will hear."

"It doesn't matter," he shouted. "Nothing matters. Not today."

The long banishment was over. Catherine had thrown her arms round him. He had Martha by the waist. Behind him lumbered a grinning Josh, most wonderfully changed.

"Chuck it over into the churchyard, Josh," he called back to him, referring to his red-spotted bundle of clothes. "We'll pick it up on our way back."

"Why, where are we going?" Martha asked.

He stopped and gazed into the gray eyes that had been haunting him.

"Where would you like to go?" he asked eagerly. "Shall we hire a boat? Walk up to Grisedale? Anything. Just say."

Martha frowned and turned away.

What had he done? She seemed angry with him.

"But aren't you tired?" broke in Catherine. "Don't you want to go home . . . and . . . and eat something?"

"Oh, Catherine, *please*," he flashed irritably. "Don't condemn me to Aunt Biddy's dreary face any sooner than you've got to."

"It should be Josh's day," said Martha firmly. "Let *him* choose."

"Yes," said Catherine eagerly, drawing Josh into discussion.

"You choose, Josh. What would *you* most like to do?"

Stephen looked at this new brother of his again, marveling at the change, seeing that Josh was no longer a gangling boy but almost a grown man.

"G-go up to the t-tarn," he burst out in confusion.

Stephen saw on the instant that though it was Catherine who was asking him, it was Martha whom Josh answered. Josh's quick flush revealed his plight.

Dear Heaven help us! he thought with an amused smile, as he swept Josh on ahead with him along the margin of the lake. Had she bewitched him, too?

He asked him then about his life at sea. Was he happy? Had he made friends? What was Uncle Parkin like as a captain? And he listened to the stammered replies with only half his mind, so perturbed was he to discover that Josh thought himself old enough to be in love with a girl.

"What exactly do you do on board, Josh? What are your duties?" he asked absently.

Josh told him.

Unlucky idiot that he was! The answer made Stephen laugh.

"Have you heard anything like it?" he called back gaily to the girls walking behind them. "Uncle Parkin takes a couple of goats and a lot of hens to sea with him. And poor old Josh, as midshipman, has to clean up their mess!"

Josh looked furious.

"Well, what of it?" asked Martha sharply. "If he stayed at home and became a farmer, he'd do the same—and you wouldn't think it strange!"

"Yes," he dashed on heedlessly, "but for the East India Company to dress him up in a scarlet waistcoat and breeches and give him a commission just to clean up after a couple of goats and some hens! It's ridiculous!"

"He does a lot of other things, too," burst out Martha angrily.

"In any case," said Catherine, laughing, "it's no more ridiculous than you wearing that stupid cap and gown at Oxford in order to sit down and read a book."

Josh bellowed with laughter.

The joke was certainly on himself, he thought ruefully, laughing too.

They walked on as before, Stephen and Josh in front and the two girls talking and laughing some thirty feet behind. Not a breath of wind stirred in the summer trees; the lake at their side stretched gleaming and without ripples to the farther shore, where, above the oak woods, High Dod and Place Hill raised their heads to an azure sky. It was a day of unparalleled peace.

Stephen looked across the quiet lake and sighed with contentment. What did it matter that he had just made a fool of himself? He was home again in the hills where he belonged. And Josh was at his side. Josh, whom Martha had just defended with such fierceness! Josh, now worthy of respect!

He turned to his brother again, this time with real interest, and asked him about his prospects. Had he truly any chance of making his fortune one day?

"A m-modest c-c-competence. Not a f-fortune," he replied.

And Josh went on—pleased by his brother's concern—to tell him about the officers' private trading and the increased tonnage they were allowed with each promotion in rank.

"And you will get promotion?"

"Uncle P-Parkin thinks I'm all right," Josh grinned happily with a modest flush. "He's rec-commended me for fourth mate. If I g-go on d-doing all right, I'll be third mate by the t-time I'm t-twenty-one, and—and first mate t-two or three years later."

"And with a first mate's tonnage?" he asked, fascinated by the simplicity of it all.

"I m-might be able to earn enough to b-buy my f-farm!"

Stephen smiled at such unpretentious hopes.

"I'm glad *one* member of the family seems likely to get his heart's desire," he said.

"But won't *you*?" asked the startled Josh. "C-Catherine says you're d-doing wonderfully well at Oxford—now that you've s-settled down."

He smiled at the lie—and at the teller of it, too.

Then, he frowned.

Their damned uncles wanted to turn him into a parson, Stephen reminded his brother. And he could not be a parson. He could not swear to the Thirty-nine Articles. He did not believe in them.

"Wh-what will you do?"

"God knows!" he sighed, puzzled.

They had left the highway now, turning away from the lake onto the pack road that wound up Grisedale Valley to the tarn.

"T-tell me about France," Josh burst out.

"Do you really want to know?" he asked eagerly.

"Of c-course!"

So Stephen told him. He told him of his setting out with John Taverner across the vast plain of northern France and of his leaving his friend at the crossroads. He described to him the poverty and strange terror of the people of St. Gilles and—without blinking at the details—recounted the sacking of the *château*, the violence, the bloodshed, the drunken rejoicing. He was as frank with his brother as he had been with Tristram Walkinshaw.

Josh suddenly stopped dead in the middle of the mountain path.

"And you m-made *friends* with such m-monsters!" he burst out in consternation.

They were not monsters, he replied impatiently. They were poor peasants who had long been cruelly ill used.

"They're *Frenchmen*," Stephen cried passionately. "As much *men* as ourselves!"

"We d-don't smash out p-people's brains," roared Josh. "Or hack down old women when we're d-drunk. We *don't,* Stephen!"

"We will—if we come to suffer like the people of St. Gilles."

"But we won't. We've got j-just laws."

"No, we haven't, you fool!"

Catherine was suddenly standing between them.

"Stop it! Stop it! *Stop* it!" she stormed at them both. "This is not India. And it isn't France. It's *England!* Besides, it's our first day together. It's our very first!"

She was choking with anger and disappointment.

They stood there in silence, glaring at each other, Stephen's heart thudding painfully in the shock of their sudden quarrel.

"It's not only England," said Martha quietly. "It's Grisedale . . . and . . . and it's beautiful."

Slowly the hills came about him again. He heard the song of a lark and the tumbling of the brook.

Without a word, he left them and ran down to the gully.

Leaping upstream from rock to rock, deafened by the water's roar, he slowly came to himself.

Poor, stupid Josh! he thought. What did he know about life— shut up in his miserable ship? What did anyone in England know about wretchedness—who had not seen St. Gilles?

Back at Town End that night, he was shown the Indian shawls that Josh had brought home for the girls.

They were beautiful.

They were warm and light and woven in the most lovely patterns that he had ever seen.

"Dear Heavens," he thought sadly, as he fingered their softness yet once again. "And I have come to her bearing no gifts!"

He kept stealing glances at his sister's friend, trying to guess the mind that lay behind so grave and charming a face. But Martha was not expansive, like Catherine. He could not tell by looking at her what would touch her heart.

In the steady rain of the next two days, he tried poetry. He took his favorite poets to the window seat where Martha sat sewing to get the best of the gray light, and began reading to her the poems that he liked best. Catherine sat beside them, her hands idle in her lap. Josh sat by the hearth staring owlishly at the *Camberstock Clarion*.

He tried moving Martha with Marvell and George Herbert and Henry Vaughan. But she sat on quietly sewing with the same small smile on her lips. Then he tried Milton's sonnet on his blindness and, looking up—all aglow—found her biting off a thread.

Perhaps the seventeenth century seemed too remote to her, he thought, running up to his attic to fetch down a small volume of verse that he had just bought in Oxford.

He came down and astonished the farmhouse parlor with poems about a chimney sweep and a black boy and about the charity children of London filing into St. Paul's for their annual service of thanksgiving on Holy Thursday.

He ended quietly, made quiet himself by the poet's wide and all-embracing love:

> *Can I see another's woe,*
> *And not be in sorrow too?*
> *Can I see another's grief,*
> *And not seek for kind relief?*

"Oh, Stephen!" cried Catherine, her eyes streaming with tears. "Who could have written such lines?"

"William Blake," he replied absently, gazing heartbroken at the placid Martha. "A London engraver. People say he's mad."

Josh let out a boisterous laugh, threw down the *Camberstock Clarion,* and banged out of the room.

Catherine lay in bed that night aching for her two brothers—and yet overtaken every now and again by inexplicable gusts of laughter.

They were both in love with her friend, she thought. And Martha—for all she knew—had not a thought in her head for either of them.

6

Paris

During 1791, the uneasy calm in France showed signs of coming to an end. The National Assembly confiscated the property of the Church and decreed that in the future all parish priests and bishops should be elected by the citizens. King Louis XVI, a deeply religious man, knowing himself to be a virtual prisoner in his own capital, decided to flee to the eastern frontier and to put himself at the head of a loyal army awaiting him there, ready to invade France to restore the old order of government. At midnight on Tuesday, June 21, the Royal Family fled from the Tuileries—and, twenty-three hours later, were overtaken and captured at Varennes. They were brought back to Paris to face a vast crowd thronging their route, crying *"Vive la Nation,"* and an Assembly determined never to let them escape again.

"Well, now they can dethrone the blockhead!" Stephen exclaimed on first hearing the news.

"Not so fast. Not so fast," replied John Taverner, laughing. "The King has his uses yet."

"What uses?" he asked angrily. "How can a sovereign who is in league with his country's enemies be of any use to his countrymen?"

"Like it or not, you hothead, the King of France still has the blind loyalty of many of his subjects."

"After fleeing to Varennes?"

"I think so. We shall see."

Stephen wanted to go and see that same summer. He wanted to go to Paris and stand in the crowd; wanted to feel what it was like to be a Frenchman in these troubled times.

But both he and Taverner were out of money. Besides, their University examinations were upon them in the coming months.

So he had to wait, biting his nails and studying his Greek and Latin texts all that summer and autumn and winter, while political events in Paris grew harder and harder to follow, and while France's enemies gathered on its frontiers with one aim in mind: to rescue the beleaguered King.

In April, the Legislative Assembly declared war on Austria.

All that early summer of 1792, he watched the fortunes of revolutionary France in an agony of suspense. The war was going badly. There were riots in the big cities. Wild bands roamed the countryside.

And—while he watched—he found that he had won a college prize worth thirty pounds!

"Now we can go!" he shouted excitedly, flinging himself into Taverner's room. "I've got the money. You get something out of your father."

"To France? But the country's at war!"

"What better time?" he cried exultantly. "It's in danger! The freedom of the world is in danger! What better time to go to its help?"

It was on the tenth of August that Stephen first heard men singing *La Marseillaise*. It was at Breteuil-sur-Noye, just before dawn. The marvelous lilt of the song came to him between sleeping and waking from a long way off—out in the fields, in the darkness. Were the reapers busy so early in the harvest fields? he wondered, propping himself up on his elbows. But now that he was wide awake, he knew that no reaper could swing his scythe to such an urgent beat. It was too headlong. Too full of joy.

Then, as he lay listening, he heard the tramp of many men's feet. Soldiers! That was it! Soldiers marching to the frontier!

He jumped out of bed and ran to the inn window, unfastened

the latch and looked down into the hot and empty square of the little town. The houses were in darkness, every window shuttered. A white scarf of mist trailed beneath the plane trees. As he stared at the mist, the singing grew closer and clearer. He could almost catch the words. He shivered. He had never heard such a song. The joy of it caught at his throat.

"Listen!" he called back to his companion. "Listen to them singing!"

John Taverner stirred, turned over in bed, and then rose sleepily and joined him at the casement. The men approaching them through the gray light must have come now to the first cobbles, for their boots rang on the stones. At the rising swell of their voices and the sharp clump of their boots, the town of Breteuil at last roused itself from its slumbers and threw open its windows.

> *Allons, enfants de la patrie,*
> *Le jour de gloire est arrivé!*

sang out a young man's voice.

At that moment, the singers themselves appeared. The first soldiers had entered the shadowy street. He could see the glint and swing of their arms and a man waving his nightcap as they passed. On and on they came, filling the street, their first column now winding across the square; their voices, channeled and caught up between the houses, growing louder and louder, until suddenly the rooftops rang to the thunderous burst of their chorus:

> *Aux armes, citoyens!*

Stephen leaned far out of the bedroom window and gazed down in astonishment at the eager and undisciplined soldiers of revolutionary France swinging past below him.

Rank upon rank of shabby infantrymen swung by, tense-faced, sweating, and pale in the first light; a hundred—two hundred—

three—he could no longer count them. All the while the soldiers sang: "To arms, citizens! To arms!" and the people cheered.

When the last column had passed through the little town, and the square was empty and the windows shut again—and Taverner had gone trailing back to bed—he stayed on where he was, gazing into the hot dawn and listening to the clumping boots and the wonderful song dying away eastwards towards Montdidier.

The day of glory had indeed come—or else the day of defeat. The *émigrés,* led by the King's brother, and the Prussian and Austrian armies were massed on the frontiers. Russia, Spain, and Sardinia threatened to mobilize, too. The whole of Europe—save Britain—seemed bent on killing the Revolution.

The two of them had been deep in the country—at St. Gilles— since the end of July. It was only that morning at breakfast that they learned of the Duke of Brunswick's manifesto.

"Ah yes, brave fellows!" sighed the innkeeper, referring to the soldiers. "Our lives are in their hands."

"The future of the Revolution lies with its army," agreed Taverner in his polished French.

"No, monsieur. The future of *ourselves!* If the Prussians win the battle, they will kill us."

"Come, man," protested Taverner. "You are a civilian."

"Why!" exclaimed the innkeeper. "Have you not heard?"

"Heard what?" they both asked.

"Their commander . . . the Duke of Brunswick . . ."

The Prussian commander-in-chief, he said, had threatened to put the people of Paris to the sword should the least harm come to the King or to the Royal Family.

"And if they kill the people of Paris, monsieur—why should they stop at killing us?"

"Paris must protect the King!" exclaimed Taverner, white in the face.

"*Nom de Dieu!*" burst out the innkeeper. "You are a stranger, monsieur. You do not know the people of Paris. The manifesto . . . it has sent them mad!"

"This is no time to go to Paris," Taverner said, turning quickly to Stephen. "Let us turn back!"

"No!" he flashed back. "Are you frightened by this fellow's tale? Are you a coward? No harm has yet come to the King— and we have paid for our *fiacre*."

They drove on towards the great city, as they had planned, but were halted by a large crowd at St. Just, thronging the street, listening to their mayor reading out the news.

"Something has happened!" exclaimed Stephen's panic-stricken fellow revolutionary.

The fool! Of course something had happened! The towns-people all about them were speechless with excitement. In the tense silence, the voice of the mayor came to the two of them, sitting in the *fiacre*.

"The city is in turmoil," Taverner translated quickly. "Drummers are beating the call to arms. They have called out the National Guard."

"Why?" Stephen whispered hoarsely. "The enemy—surely they've not reached Paris already?"

"No," muttered his companion. "It is the *fédérés*—the revolutionary bands who have marched north from Marseilles—and the people from the slums of St. Antoine . . . they are marching on the Tuileries."

"The palace?"

Taverner nodded—and turned back to the mayor.

"The Commune . . . fears a plot," he muttered, translating freely as the speaker went on. "They are sounding the tocsin . . ."

"A plot? What kind of plot?"

"They say the King is in league with the Prussians."

"Long live the Nation!" bawled the mayor, coming to the end of his paper.

"Now we *can't* go on!" Taverner rounded on his companion. "The King's life is in danger. If they kill him—and their army is defeated—we'll be butchered along with the rest of the city."

Stephen saw the terror in his eyes and was filled with contempt.

"If . . . if," he gibed cruelly. And then added, more reasonably: "The National Guard will protect the King!"

"For how long?" his companion flared at him. "The whole city's at the mercy of the mob."

The *fiacre* moved on with a jolt.

"It'll be the King's death we'll hear of next," groaned the wretched Taverner.

"What of it? He's only mortal. He's got to die sometime."

"But not like this!"

Stephen shrugged his shoulders. "Much better to clear away all the old rubbish—and start again," he grinned.

"With the imperial armies on the frontier?"

"What braver moment to declare a republic?"

They were out in the country now, and—seeing the number of carriages, cabriolets, and coaches speeding towards them out of the capital—Taverner's panic burst out anew. It was *mad* of them to drive on into Paris. They had work to do in England. Important work. They must carry on the Revolution at home.

"What good will it do our country's cause to get ourselves killed in the Paris streets?"

"*Our* country?" Stephen shouted back, over the rattle of the wheels. "We have no country. We belong to the race of men."

At Chantilly, where they stopped to bait the horses, the ostler told them exactly what had happened. The King and the Royal Family had fled from the palace in the early hours of the morning and thrown themselves upon the mercy of the deputies then sitting in debate in the National Assembly. The Swiss Guard had opened fire on the enraged people who had attempted to storm the palace, and the mob—in turn—had brought up guns and slaughtered the Swiss Guard.

"Now we *must* stop!" burst out John Taverner. "We *can't* go on!"

But it was all over, Stephen urged. The crisis had passed. The danger was behind them. What they had worked for all their lives had come about. A king had fallen! The first of the tyrants of Europe! How could they possibly turn back now? Why—could not he see—*a new age* had dawned!

"Drive on!" he shouted exultantly to their driver.

They entered the great city through the Faubourg St. Denis. Stephen looked about him with the greatest excitement. But he was disappointed. The streets were quiet. There were very few people about.

"It looks as though they've all gone off to some fair!" he exclaimed in chagrin.

"Perhaps they have!" answered Taverner grimly.

Now they were through the old city walls. And here, at last, both the houses and the people seemed to crowd quickly about them. Women craned out of the windows of the tall tenements towering above their heads; the dusty lanes on either side of them were thronged with citizens wearing revolutionary scarves. One-horse cabs and tumbrils dashed among the pedestrians; men shouted and scattered; women shrieked. Here was Paris at last! Paris in the greatest moment of the Revolution.

Stephen looked this way and that, astonished at the number of soldiers and the fierce aspect of the ragged men who had come north from Marseilles. He saw an Arab in a white burnous and a huge Negro with a shining face. And here, now, was a striding six-footer who must surely be an American. This was not just Paris. It was the heart of the world.

"Set us down at the Rue St. Honoré," Taverner shouted to the driver.

Stephen turned to him in surprise. They had taken lodgings, he knew, across the river in the Faubourg St. Germain.

"Yes, I know," replied his companion, a little awkwardly. "But we can walk the rest of the way. We . . . we can walk past the Tuileries . . . and . . . and the National Assembly . . . and cross the river to our lodging by the Port Royal."

Stephen turned away, grinning. He knew little about Paris, but that little was enough for him to understand that his fainthearted friend wanted to gape at the empty palace and to stare at the walls of the building where the fallen King was lodged.

And why not? They were only hours behind the greatest event of modern times.

The driver set them down in a more gracious part of the city. Here, the buildings all looked like palaces. There was space here. And light. And fine trees. They found their boots crushing crisp brown leaves and saw ahead of them a street cleaner sweeping them up into tidy piles.

A short burst of musket fire sputtered some quarter of a mile away.

More trouble?

A passerby shrugged his shoulders and walked on. The sweeper continued his sweeping. All down the long avenue, Stephen could see the old fellow's day's work: the piles of dead leaves, casting their small shadows in the westering light.

Beneath the walls of the Tuileries Gardens, they came upon a knot of people gathered round something lying on the ground.

"What is it?" asked Taverner of a bystander on the outside of the small crowd.

The man grinned.

"One of the murderers," he replied, letting them pass through to see for themselves.

Taverner looked and turned away quickly, clutching the garden railings. Stephen stood and stared. At their feet lay a man's naked body—without a head. There was a small black hole no bigger than a guinea piece just above the heart of the naked trunk. That was how death had come. Quickly. With a bullet. But why the nakedness? Why had they cut off the head?

Taverner twitched at his sleeve to pull him away.

"One of the Swiss Guard," he muttered, green in the face, as they moved hurriedly on.

But there was to be no easy way of escaping from the morning's horror, for approaching them creaked a large, overladen cart and, with it, a detachment of seven or eight soldiers, busy clearing up after this small but most savage of battles. Every now and again, the soldiers stopped, gathered round another dismembered corpse, then stooped, picked it up, and swung it carelessly into the back of the cart. Stephen shuddered. Every wretched Swiss guardsman had been stripped naked by the mob. Their white bodies must have lain exposed all day.

"Let's turn back," whispered Taverner.

"They were protecting a tyrant!" Stephen burst out wildly. "They fired on the people. Ordinary men and women died here last night—as well as those guardsmen!"

And where *was* this tyrant?

Taverner jerked his head absently towards a building across the avenue. A small crowd of soldiers and citizens stood at its entrance, watching a band of red-capped *fédérés* marching by to the rattle of a single drum.

He stared at the walls of the National Assembly, empty of emotion.

So this was Paris! This was what one had to endure to depose a king.

Next morning, Stephen had recovered somewhat from his shock. Leaving his exhausted companion still sleeping, he crept down the lodging stairs into the first light.

All Paris lay before him.

Cocks were crowing in distant yards. There was a smell of bread baking. Though it was scarcely yet day, the women of the Faubourg St. Germain were already opening their windows and throwing garbage down into the gutters. He did not know his way. But he was not a fool. He looked up at the ribbon of sky between the high roofs and, seeing the faint color in the east, struck out in the direction of the Seine. In the Rue de Sèvres, he dodged his way among the early vegetable carts and made for the Pont Neuf.

Here was the river, at last, and the great cathedral of Notre Dame far to his right; and, far to his left across the water, the

quay and the palace and the gardens where the two of them had
walked the evening before. A faint mist lay over the river. It was
going to be hot again.

Everything that he saw that first early morning filled him with

delight. The sun rose into the clearest of skies, and the water of
the Seine sparkled and, in its quieter reaches, slowly took on the
color of the sky. The great buildings and the bridges and the
trees, as though swept clean by the disappearing mist, stood noble
and distinct. Yet, it was the *people* he met—rather than the view
—that gave him such joy. They looked cheerful; confident; gay.
They walked with a purpose; they had jobs to do. A man tossed
a joke to a neighbor across the bridge. Both laughed. Catching
some of their Gallic verve as he sniffed the morning anew, it
seemed impossible to him that he and Taverner had really seen
what they had the night before.

As he drifted into the Rue St. Denis, he realized that most of
the citizens were hurrying in a single direction: into the Rue St.
Honoré. Some of them were carrying ropes and tackle; they were
shouting to one another, issuing instructions in a jocular holiday
mood. He found himself drawn along behind them—cheerfully
curious. They passed a wide, open space on the right, surrounded
with booths and bookstalls and little tents where one could buy
food. The smell of hot rolls sharpened his hunger. But he was
caught up by this infectiously good-tempered early-morning
crowd and was, indeed, now hemmed in from behind by rougher

and more vociferous citizens who had joined them from some suburb to the east. There was no escape for him—even if he had wished it.

"We'll pull the tyrant down today," came a shout from behind him. "We failed yesterday. But we'll make him bite the dust today."

Ropes? Tackle? He was suddenly appalled. Was this cheerful, laughing crowd marching to hang its King? Sucked onwards by the throng, he saw that the mob—and he with it—was now turning right and debouching into an enormous square. They had left the National Assembly, and the Royal Family inside it, way behind them. He sighed with relief. The King could be executed, for all he cared. But solemnly. By law. Not by a mob with ropes.

Once well out into the open space, the first rank of citizens let out a great shout. They had been forestalled!

Peering over their shoulders, he saw a fierce woman up on horseback—splendid in a soldier's scarlet coat—who was commanding men in the placing of ropes about a great equestrian statue. The ropes were already taut round the necks of man and horse.

That was it!

This huge crowd of people had gathered in the square to tear down—a statue! He could hear the sharp hammering of chisels against the heavy plinth. He could see men and women fighting for a place in the lines of heaving, tugging citizens bent on rocking down the proud figure mounted on its charger.

The great king shuddered.

"Le Roi Soleil!" jeered a man beside him, as the mighty statue of horse and king swayed drunkenly from side to side.

He watched spellbound as Louis XIV—the greatest king of France—raised high above the people, silently bowed to their power in the cool morning air.

Then, with a rending and splintering of stone, the figure toppled slowly to the left and came crashing down with a crack of thunder on the paving stones.

Up went a roar. A triumphant yell of ferocious joy from a thousand throats surged on and on—like a river in spate—seeming to flood the whole world.

"Where the hell have you been?" Taverner flared at him when he got back to their lodging.

"Out in the streets."

"You're not safe—alone—in this place."

"Who wants to be *safe?*" he jeered.

"You should have waited for me. I know the language. I know my way about."

"My God, man!" he replied angrily. "You are not my keeper."

"No, thank Heaven!" came the furious reply. "I'm only your countryman."

Two days later, he and Taverner stood among the crowd lining the royal route from the National Assembly to the Temple. The Paris Commune could not contain its joy. King Louis XVI, his hated Queen, and their two children were being driven away from the protection of the deputies—to prison. Women, running along to keep level with the carriages, howled out their execrations upon the cold eyes, the proud face, the ruined beauty they saw sitting beside their fallen King.

"Harlot!" they yelled. "Whore!"

"Poor woman!" sighed Stephen's confused companion when they were safely back in the privacy of their lodging. "One's heart bleeds for her."

"For *Marie Antoinette?* For *that* heartless creature?"

"But she's a *woman!* How dreadful for her to be taunted by such scum!"

"Scum?" shouted Stephen. "How can you say such a thing? They are human beings like ourselves!"

"Do we shout 'Whore!' at a fallen queen?"

"No, but ours has not laughed at us when our children starved."

He was suddenly overcome with contempt for this sentimental, muddleheaded, fainthearted friend of his. He turned on him, demandingly scornfully:

"Did I see *you* showing your concern for the woman just now in the open street?"

Taverner had, indeed, watched the Royal Family being driven away to prison with an expression on his face as stony as his friend's.

"How *could* I?" he whipped out, both exasperated and ashamed. "They'd have knocked us down—hanged us both on the next lamppost."

"Oh, come, come," Stephen taunted him. "You could have told them we were English."

This had, in fact, saved them from trouble only the day before.

They had been walking across the Place du Carousel early in the evening, when a red-capped youth, after eyeing Taverner's good broadcloth and the smart English cut of his coat, had suddenly yelled out:

"Here's an aristocrat! An aristocrat!"

In a moment, they had been surrounded by a crowd of angry citizens, clenching their fists and spitting in their faces. They would have done worse had not Taverner, white with panic, shouted out over the hubbub:

"We are English! English students. English friends of the Revolution."

Suiting action to words, he had flung up his right arm and cried: *"Vive la Nation! Vive la Nation!"*

And the red-capped *fédérés* had immediately clapped them on the shoulders, shaken their hands, and sent them on their way with every mark of friendliness and accord.

The incident, however, had so much frightened Stephen's elegant Oxford companion that, on returning to their lodging, he had stripped off his good English coat and had insisted upon borrowing a spare one of Stephen's made years ago by the Camberstock tailor, which was now threadbare at the elbows.

"Yes," he taunted his friend again. "You could have told the mob when they slung the rope round your neck . . . that you were English and hated tyrants as much as they. Only . . . only that you had an unaccountable weakness for queens!"

"You're a fool, Parkin!" Taverner shouted at him. "God knows why I ever consented to come with you to this dreadful place!"

Yet, against all reason, they stayed on together, watchful of each other's tempers, like two wary dogs. They stayed on in the turbulent city—because it was unthinkable to leave it. They were witnessing—so they thought—the most extraordinary events in the history of the world.

While the revolutionary armies marched singing to the frontier, and the factions raged in the streets, they walked about Paris, their minds agape. They stood in the old Palais Royal Gardens listening to a street orator denouncing Louis Bourbon as a traitor. A traitor to his country. Papers had been found in the palace. There had been a plot. A plot between the Court and the enemy now crossing the frontier.

"Death to the tyrant!" howled their neighbors standing in the crowd. "Death to the Queen!"

Then they strolled away, the two of them, and wandered in the Champs Elysées, staring in astonishment at the citizens laughing at the pantomimes and the performing animals and drinking and making merry at the refreshment booths under the trees.

And then—quite suddenly—it was no longer safe to be an Englishman.

"They've recalled our ambassador," gasped a white-faced John Taverner on returning to their lodging one night, having been out by himself.

The British Government—slow of hearing—had at last been made aware of the storming of the Tuileries Palace and the butchery of the Swiss Guard and of the imprisonment of the Royal Family. It had ordered Lord Gower, the British ambassador, to leave Paris and return home.

"The students round the bookstalls say that Great Britain is about to join France's enemies," he panted.

"I don't believe it!" Stephen exclaimed.

"Nor do I. But that's not the point. *They* do. They say our Government has filled the city with its spies."

"Spies? How absurd!"

"Not to them. They've got proof."

"What proof?"

"Paris is full of English guinea pieces. It's money sent over for bribes, they say."

Stephen roared with laughter. He had never heard such nonsense.

"Not even the British Government," he declared, "is as idiotic as *that!*"

"It's no laughing matter, you fool," his frightened companion flared at him. "Don't you see, it won't be safe for us any longer in the streets."

"All right," he said, surveying him lazily. "Let's go home. We've seen enough."

Yet, getting home soon proved far more difficult than either realized.

Next morning, they presented themselves at the passport office and were told that no passes were being issued to strangers. The country was in danger; the fate of the armies uncertain; the city in a turmoil.

"I am sorry, *messieurs,* you must stay here in Paris—till better times."

But the better times did not come.

All through those stifling last days of August, rumors—terrible rumors of defeat on the frontier—swept the city. The factions raged. Drums rattled. The tocsin sounded the alarm.

Stephen, wandering again through the Champs Elysées, stared with new wonder at the citizens still dancing and singing under the trees.

What a nation! he thought, his astonishment mingled with awe.

His companion, however, was too frightened to notice anything but fresh grounds for his terror.

"They're imprisoning the priests and all aristocrats left in the city," he whispered, as they stood by one of the booths drinking wine. With his better French, the chance word, the secret look, the dreadful undercurrent of fear and suspicion did not pass him by. "The prisons are crammed with people awaiting trial."

Stephen accepted this calmly. The Revolution was facing its supreme test.

And then—on the thirty-first of August—without warning, came the event that shipwrecked his life.

The two of them entered a wide square in a part of the city that was new to them. There were soldiers at the far end of it and an excited crowd gathered round a low platform, shouting at someone out of sight.

"What's happening?" Stephen asked, striding across the square to see what was up.

"It's not our business," urged his timid friend, clutching at his arm. "Let's keep away."

Everything was their business, he snapped, as he shook himself free and began threading through the knot of bystanders.

Stretched out on a hurdle lay a rough country fellow with his arms secured above his head, his feet tied wide apart, and his rags filthily blotched with the bad eggs and tomatoes with which the angry crowd had pelted him.

"Murderer! Villain! Cheat!" yelled his tormentors.

"What has he done?" asked Stephen. "Whom has he killed?"

He could not tear his gaze away from the defiant face of the man stretched out on the hurdle. It had a resolute obstinacy that was, somehow, familiar to him.

"What crime has he committed?" he asked again.

The man beside him shrugged his shoulders. He did not know. But a man immediately behind him was better informed. The rascal was a wagoner, he explained, convicted of bringing sacks of wheat into the city which were grossly under weight.

"He has killed no one?"

"He has cheated the poor."

He looked again at the unrepentant creature exposed to the taunts of the crowd.

"What are you going to do with him?" he asked the man behind him.

"Why, nothing. He has been sentenced to ten years' imprisonment."

"Then why is he here?"

"Do you not think he deserves our contempt?"

Some of the onlookers were now spitting at the wretch; others were poking him with their staves and shouting, *"Vive la Nation! Vive la République!"* bullying their victim to repeat their loyal cry himself.

Instead, the wagoner, his eyes blazing with a crazy animal courage, fixed them all with a wild creature's stubborn scorn.

Stephen's heart suddenly missed a beat. He was back in Camberstock . . . Matthew Baldry . . . standing behind his closed gate . . . defying the Duke.

"Vive la Nation!" shouted a savage *fédéré,* jabbing his stave into the corner of the wagoner's mouth and drawing blood.

Suddenly, the prisoner roared like a mad bull. His eyes rolled. He clenched his fists.

"Vive le Roi!" he yelled crazily. *"Vive la Reine!"*

Stephen gasped. The man must have gone mad. How could he shout, "Long live the King! Long live the Queen!" at such a time? It was death to him.

A great roar of rage went up from the crowd. Men were scrambling onto the platform and shrieking, *"Vive la Nation!"* into his face. And the man, his eyes no longer rolling, leered up at them and, with the obstinacy of an idiot, bawled back at them, *"Vive le Roi!"*

They were tearing now at the ropes that secured his hands. They were going to kill him. Stephen was sure they were going to kill him.

He leaped up onto the platform and flung the nearest citizen down to the cobbles.

"The man is not a traitor," he shouted in his quaint Picardy French. "He cares nothing for the King!"

There was a moment's pause before the great wave of the crowd's anger crashed over his head.

"I know his kind," he gabbled. "He is a *peasant*. You have

taunted him. He defies you. He will say anything . . . *anything* that is the opposite of what you want him to say."

There was a split second of utter silence. The sun stood in the sky. A cloud like a small pillow sat over a church spire. On the far side of the great square an Englishman in a familiar threadbare coat was hurrying away.

And then, with the roar of rocks crashing down a mountainside, the crowd hurled itself on the platform. A man seized his arms and held them in an iron grip behind his back. Another leaped up in front of him and smashed his fist into his face.

"Don't kill the fellow," shouted a stentorian voice over the clamor. *"Arrest* him!"

7

The Prison

It was very early. Very silent. And it was Sunday.

He opened his eyes and stared at the motes of dust streaming in a shaft of sunlight far above his head. He knew where he was. In prison. His terrible plight had haunted his dreams. He was lying on the floor of a great chamber together with an aristocrat, a priest, a Paris lawyer, a bookseller, a printer, and a half-wit—all royalists—who knew themselves marked for death.

It had been dusk two evenings earlier when he had first been thrown in among these people. They had gathered round him to comfort him in his disaster. The young nobleman had saluted him; the gaunt lawyer had nodded to him; the priest had blessed him. The bookseller and the printer had shaken him by the hand. The half-wit pickpocket had kept to his corner and grinned.

"We are all condemned to die, my son," the old priest had said quietly. "Like the rest of us, you must make your peace with God."

"Condemned?" he had gasped. "But why?"

"Because the prisons are full of us," groaned the printer.

"I do not understand!"

The citizen armies were marching out to save Verdun, the lawyer had explained, leaving Paris without troops and with hundreds of the Commune's enemies shut up in its prisons.

"We are too many to leave alive!" the bookseller had cried out in anguish.

"But *I* am not condemned," Stephen had protested. "I have not even been tried."

The half-wit had broken out in a high, hysterical laugh.

"Not one of us has been tried, my poor provincial," the lawyer had replied. "Yet, all of us are dead men."

"But I am not an enemy of the Commune!" he had burst out. "I am its *friend!*"

They had stared at him in amazement then. Slowly, in ones and twos, they had turned from him in silence.

He had spent the early hours of that terrible first night alone— more utterly alone than he had ever been in his life. His ribs had been so pommeled by the crowd that he could not lie down. He had sat up in the darkness, leaning against the wall, wondering where he had gone wrong. What had he *done?* He had tried to save a fool—an idiot too stupid to save himself. Was it not right to save simple people? Tormented people? Was this not what the Revolution was all about? Besides, how could he have left that poor devil, crucified on his hurdle? He had looked at Stephen with eyes that he knew. Through the wagoner's eyes, all the shepherds and tinkers of Westmorland had demanded his help.

In the darkness, the old priest had come to give him comfort.

"Alas, my poor boy," he had murmured. "Why did you leave your village?"

"But, Father, I am not a French villager!" he had exclaimed in astonishment. "I am English! An English student! An English friend of the Revolution!"

"English?" the nobleman had barked, somewhere in the shadows. "The more fool you to betray so good a land!"

And now it was Sunday. And there was silence.

As he lay there, watching the motes in the sunbeam, his former life passed headlong before him: his father's death; Catherine;

Josh; his battles with his uncles; Ellenhead and his wild escapades; Oxford; Taverner; St. Gilles; the Paris streets. His breakneck career had come to a full stop, here in this prison and this silence, lying on this filthy straw!

Then the bells began ringing again in the Paris belfries, and he lay listening to them, wondering absently why he was so certain that it must be Sunday. It was not the bells. They were summoning men to arms, not to prayer. They had been clanging out the tocsin in this way every few hours since the morning of his arrest, warning the city of its danger. The enemy threatened Verdun. If Verdun were taken, then the road lay open to Paris. The clamor of the tocsin, the rattle of drums, the cries of *"Aux armes, citoyens!"* and the tramp of many feet in the street outside had come to them all the day before in this dark and waiting place—thinly, like the sounds of life seeping through a graveyard to the dead.

He shivered.

Sunday. The *smell* of Sunday—Sunday in the tiny parish church at St. Gilles. That was it!

Very cautiously—because of his bruised ribs—he turned himself on the straw and gazed down the length of the great chamber.

The early morning light, pouring through the high lancet windows, stretched in four level bars across the upper air; but below, on the floor, the sleeping prisoners still lay in shadow. Yet, as his eyes grew sharper in the grayness, he saw that one of his companions was not asleep. He was kneeling on a kind of low dais at the far end of the room, his face to the wall. A faint curl of smoke hung in a wreath above his head. Incense! The old priest was saying his prayers. He leaned up on his elbow and gazed at the kneeling figure, catching now for the first time the faint mumble of Latin. He followed a wisp of smoke weaving upwards to unwind itself in the farthest bar of light, and suddenly thought how strange it was that he—a northerner, a revolutionary, and a near-atheist—should be lying here at such a time

watching a Romish priest preparing himself for death. It moved him, in spite of himself. There were worse ways of getting ready for one's end.

Then he sat up in a hurry. His ears had caught other sounds besides the ringing of bells and the shouts and cries coming distantly from the street. He could hear the tramp of boots and the sharp rap of orders within the prison itself.

The door of the great chamber shook as the heavy key was turned in its massive lock.

Their jailer stood looking down upon them all.

"Wake yourselves, sirs!" he bawled. "Verdun has fallen. This morning the Commune orders that you be brought to your trials."

It flashed through his mind that his nightmare was over. They were going to be tried properly—before a judge.

"Monsieur le Vicomte," continued the jailer. "You are to come to the court first."

"Now?" asked the nobleman, scrambling up from the floor.

"Immediately. The court awaits you."

Snatched so suddenly out of his sleep, Stephen watched him falter.

"My lawyer . . . is he here? Has he come . . . so early?"

The jailer shrugged his shoulders.

"Speak, man," rasped the lawyer. "The defendant has a right by law to be defended at his trial."

Behind the jailer stood two common soldiers who were acting as the prisoners' escort.

"Why, an innocent man, 'e don't need no lawyer to speak for 'im," exclaimed one of the soldiers.

" 'E can speak for hisself," jeered the other.

A silent panic swept the chamber.

The nobleman straightened himself, held out his hand in a brief farewell to those immediately about him, and then turned and knelt at the priest's side.

"Hurry along with you," grumbled the jailer. "The court hasn't got all day."

Stephen watched the old priest rise to his feet, make the sign of the cross, and bless the man going to his death. Then the Vicomte got up quickly and walked the length of the prison chamber, head held high, looking neither to right nor to left, smiling a little as though he were about to meet friends.

When he came to the jailer, he wheeled round suddenly and faced them all.

"Long live the King!" he said resolutely. "Long live the glory of France!"

Stunned by his going, they stood listening to the footsteps of the Vicomte and his escort echoing down the passage to some more distant part of the prison, their horror slowly mounting in the silent chamber—until it spilled over in a startling scream.

"Speak for *myself!*" shrieked the crazed pickpocket. "I . . . I cannot speak for myself! I am . . . a poor . . . poor ignorant fool!"

Sick of heart and as frightened as any, Stephen listened to the poor devil's countrymen, pent up with their own terror, turning upon him in rage. They were all in the same plight, they cried. Not one of them had prepared his defense! How could they? They did not know with what crime they were being charged. He must shut up! Stop his whining. Or they would knock his head against the wall.

Only the priest tried to help him.

"If you've done nothing more than you say you have," he murmured gently, "then they will hardly condemn you to death."

"Tell them you've only slit the pockets of the rich," snarled the bookseller, "and maybe they'll give you a medal."

Stephen sat down on his straw palliasse and clasped his head in his hands.

If the wretched thief felt the hopelessness of his case, how much worse was it for himself! He had been charged with causing a riot. With his uncertain knowledge of French and his miserable country accent, how could he possibly explain to his accusers why he had rushed to the wagoner's defense? If there was no one in the court who could speak English, he was a dead man.

He must think. *Think!* What in the name of Heaven was the French for "bravado"? "Obstinate"? "Mule"?

But, desperate though he was, he could not keep his mind on its task.

Terrible sounds were coming to him from a long way off: feet clattering down a spiral staircase; soldiers' shouts; more clattering feet; a struggle; a cry for help—and then, a long-drawn, screaming howl.

The inmates of the great chamber looked at one another in terror.

"It's . . . a man . . . *dying*," whispered the printer.

And now, from the neighboring courts of the vast prison, crept back the lesser sounds Stephen had heard earlier: the thin clang of cell doors; the distant rapping out of orders; muffled spurts of protest; a laugh; and the echoing thud of soldiers' boots.

Boots. The thud of boots.

He felt his muscles stiffen, aware suddenly that the tramp of men's feet was no longer echoing afar off but was approaching, ringingly, up the wide stairs to the door of the chamber. The guards banged to a halt. His breath caught in his chest.

"No. Not in the chapel," growled their jailer. "The prisoners on this list are lodged below—in the crypt."

Listening to the soldiers clumping back down the stairway, he gazed numbly at the old priest still kneeling where the altar should have been. Then he glanced up at the chipped face of a saint on a corbel over his head. A chapel! Of course, it was a chapel. The tall lancet windows set high in the walls should have told him as much.

From beneath the chapel floor came the dull, grating sound of bolts being drawn back, and the yawn of a door—and then the muffled tones of a voice reading out names.

They heard the sudden howl of a prisoner in the crypt below.

Stephen brushed away the sweat that was pouring down into his eyes.

The man's cry had come up to him like the startled shriek of a rabbit caught in a snare.

Soon after seven, they came for the lawyer.

He left them wordlessly, making no gesture—his face like a gray stone.

Stephen flung himself down on the straw.

It was a nightmare. He was sure it was a nightmare. At any moment he would feel himself shaken awake and open his eyes to find Catherine bending over him, her candle in her hand.

"Hush!" she would say—laughing softly, half under her breath. "Hush. You'll wake Uncle Fletcher."

And then she would put down her candle on the chest and come back to him and pass her cold hands over his forehead and stoop down and plump up his pillows.

"Smile, Stephen. Smile," she would whisper. "Don't go on looking so dreadful. It was only one of your horrid dreams."

He raised his head. A horrid dream?

In the chapel entrance stood the jailer with the soldiers. They must have issued their summons while he was lost in himself, for the old priest was standing in the middle of the chapel with his last, sad flock kneeling at his feet. He had raised his hand in benediction. Now he was moving slowly away from them towards the waiting escort.

When he came to Stephen, sitting on his palliasse, he stopped for a moment and gazed gravely into his eyes.

"May the Mother of God bring you to Christ, my son," he said, and passed on.

Appallingly, indeed, the next world was upon them, for the priest was not yet out of the door—he could still see the old man's bent shoulders between the lusty guards—when a scream, close at hand, rent the air. Then came another. And yet another. They were slaughtering the prisoners in the courtyard outside. Their dying came to the remaining occupants of the chapel in terrible, scarcely human cries.

Then, as suddenly as they had begun, they were shut off.

At the first cry from the courtyard, the bookseller had scrambled to his feet and with a yell of terror had run across the great chamber to the wide hearth and begun clawing his way up the chimney.

"No, you don't, my fine fellow," shouted one of the soldiers, plunging back into the chapel and pulling him down by the heels.

Laughing brutally, the two guards dragged the sobbing creature away behind the quiet priest.

Dumb with horror, Stephen stared at his two companions.

The pickpocket, far out on the road to madness, was rolling his head backwards and forwards against the wall. The printer was sitting hunched on the step of the dais staring down the length of the chamber—at him.

After they had gazed at each other for a time, the wizened little man got slowly to his feet and began shuffling his way between the tumbled palliasses in his direction.

"I did such a little thing . . . such a *little* thing," he sighed, as he sat down stiffly at his side.

Stephen looked at him. There was a sad sort of wonder in the printer's face.

"What did you do?" he asked.

He was a poor man, he explained. He had a wife and three children to feed. He was poor, he repeated. He could not afford to pick and choose.

"I printed . . . whatsoever men brought me to print."

Stephen frowned, puzzled for a moment.

"And some of it was seditious? Against the Commune?"

"So they say."

"Did you know that this was so?"

The printer shook his head.

"In days like these," he replied with a hopeless air, "how is it possible for a simple man to know what is permitted and what is a crime? They change these things from hour to hour."

They sat together in silence and stared at the dirty floor.

"And you?" asked his companion at length. "What did you do?"

Stephen tried to shake himself back into his senses.

"Me?"

What had he done? he sighed to himself. It seemed such a long time ago.

"I started a riot," he replied dully. "Yes. Started a riot. That's what they say."

The dreadful day dragged on and on, each hour proving more fearful than the last, for the cries of the prisoners being done to death beneath the chapel windows were coming now, not at long intervals as before, but after a silence only of minutes.

The trials must be a mockery! A quick question and answer. A last hustling down the ringing stairs. And then—a bloody dispatch.

He could not bear it. He put his hands over his ears and his head between his knees.

"If ever I come out of this . . . if ever I do . . ." he groaned to himself.

But the cries still came to him. Martha, Catherine, Josh, Mr. Walkinshaw, the hills, the mountain brooks, Milton, Shakespeare, Oxford . . . they were all swept out of his mind on the crest of the next terrible scream.

The printer left them at noon.

Only he and the pickpocket were left.

Worn out by the horror of the day and feeling himself come at last to some bleak shore sheltered from the anguish of hope, he raised his eyes and gazed at his sole companion in the chapel. The wretched thief had stopped rolling his head against the wall and was staring ahead of him with the dumb terror of a horse awaiting the Camberstock slaughterer. He quivered as a new screaming began and then, turning his eyes upon himself, suddenly seemed to feel again the terror of being a man.

With a cry for help, he stumbled across the chapel floor, flung himself at Stephen's feet, and buried his head on his knees.

Stephen put his hand on the matted hair and felt the warmth of the skull underneath. A pulse was throbbing at the side of the brow. Here was a man, like himself: one who had not asked for death. He sat there on his palliasse, stroking the filthy head, strongly moved to compassion.

"If death comes now . . . it will not come later," he murmured in English. "And if it is not to come later . . . then it will not be now."

The Paris cutpurse raised his head and held it on one side—like a puzzled dog.

Stephen stumbled out with an awkward French translation.

"But I am terrified of death," sobbed the thief. "I fear it . . . I hate it . . . *whenever* it comes!"

Then, he suddenly caught at his sobs and listened. They both listened. The escort of soldiers had come to a halt outside the door. The key turned in its lock.

"Stephen Parkin, Englishman," read out the jailer. "You are summoned to attend the court."

He looked at the crowded courtroom in horror. This was not a gathering of lawyers, but of tipsy brawlers.

"Stephen Parkin, Englishman," drawled a grating voice. "You are charged with being an enemy of the Commune."

"It is not *true*," he shouted at the cloud of tobacco smoke that hid his accuser.

"Guilty," hiccupped a soldier stretched out on a bench. "Send him down."

His numbness fell from him. He must fight. Fight.

"I am not guilty," he shouted. "I came here as your friend."

Behind him, a man laughed.

"Listen to the peasant! 'As our friend,' he says!"

"Where are his papers?" rapped out an authoritative voice, more sober than the rest.

Stephen turned to his left and caught sight of a gaunt, black-suited citizen seated at a table raised a little above the lounging throng. This, then, must be his judge. Behind him sat an older man—watchful—with an intelligent face.

The table was covered with tumbled documents, and while men

sought among them for those relating to Stephen, he took a deep breath and then, in his halting French, stammered out his brief and stupid tale. He was a friend of the Revolution, he said. He had been its friend these last three years—ever since the fall of the Bastille. This summer he had come to France, six weeks ago. He had arrived in Paris on the tenth of August . . . he had joined with the crowd that had pulled down the King's statues . . .

They had found his papers. The judge was hurriedly reading them through.

"How comes it, then," he whipped out angrily, pointing to a paragraph in the charge, "how comes it that you are arrested for defending a criminal who shouts, 'Long live the King'?"

The court roared with laughter.

"Send him down," bawled the drunken soldier on the bench.

It was a mistake, he gabbled. The court did not understand. The prisoner had not been a traitor. He had been a buffoon. A

stubborn fool. The crowd had been tormenting him. They had driven him mad. If only there was someone in the court who could understand English, he could explain it all.

"We do not understand your French, you dolt," jeered a voice from behind him, "let alone your English."

"What proof have we that you are not an English spy?" shouted another.

The court broke out in hubbub.

"He is guilty," shouted some. "Send him down," howled others. "Give him to the guards."

Only one quiet face looked at him: a common soldier seated on the floor with his back propped up against the judge's table was staring at him with a puzzled expression—almost of recognition —in his eyes.

"Order! Order!" rasped the judge, banging the table with a gavel. "We will hear the prisoner out."

In the uneasy silence that followed, Stephen found himself

gasping for words. He was like Josh. His tongue seemed locked in his mouth.

"I . . . I cannot say how it was . . . in French," he heaved out. "In England, I . . . I come from the country . . . from a farm . . ."

"We are not interested whence you come," broke in the judge impatiently, "but why . . . *why* you came to Paris . . . to France."

He had come to help Frenchmen gain their freedom, he replied brokenly.

The court was convulsed with laughter.

"What need has our great nation for a fool like you?" taunted a huge fellow from the back row.

"You had it *once!*" he flashed. "You needed me at St. Gilles! At the storming of the *château!*"

"At St. Gilles?" shouted the lout, bursting into laughter. "Where —in the name of the Devil—is St. Gilles?"

The soldier sitting on the floor slowly got to his feet.

"Citizen Dupont," he said, addressing the judge, "St. Gilles . . . there is a St. Gilles in my native Picardy . . ."

"And so?" exclaimed the judge. "Is there not a village called St. Gilles in every province in France?"

"But, citizen," said the soldier, scratching his head in perplexity, "the prisoner . . . he speaks French . . . as we do back at home. You can hear it, citizen, for yourself."

It was true. The soldier's vowels were as flat as Stephen's; his consonants were as thick.

"This *château,*" the judge said sharply, turning to Stephen. "Tell me about the storming of this *château.*"

Haltingly, he told him. He gave the exact day and month and year of its taking and described the way it was done.

The judge looked at the soldier.

"That is what my friends told me at Hesdin," the soldier said, nodding his head, ". . . that . . . an Englishman . . ."

"This fellow here . . ." laughed a citizen in derision, "*this* fellow climb the outer wall of a keep?"

"He has heard the story from others," snarled a second.

"Take him away," shouted a third. "He's a liar!"

The soldier bent his head and whispered something into the judge's ear. Citizen Dupont listened and nodded. And they whispered again.

At last, the judge looked up and addressed himself to Stephen.

"The people of Hesdin say there was an old soldier at St. Gilles —and that he, too, played a part in the taking of the *château*."

"Janvier!" he burst out eagerly. "Pierre Janvier! He was my friend!"

The judge looked at him severely.

"They say," he continued, speaking slowly and very distinctly, "that it was not the Englishman—but this soldier that first scaled the walls."

"But that is *impossible!*" he exclaimed, astounded. "Pierre Janvier has only one leg!"

In the silence that followed, he closed his eyes and thought: I am finished. This is the end. They do not believe me.

Someone scraped a chair back. He looked up. The judge had risen and was addressing the court.

"This prisoner is acquitted," he announced in a loud voice. "What he says is true. He is a hero of the Revolution!"

His triumph was terrible to him.

They scrambled down from their seats in the windows, these tipsy, fuddled men, and up from the benches and the floor and crowded round him, crying: *"Vive la Nation! Vive la République!"* They shook him by the hand, by the arm, by his shoulders. They lifted him up and chaired him out of the court, shouting, *"Vive l'Anglais!"* "This is our brother!" "He is our friend." They carried him along the echoing passageways and down the ringing stairs. Then they set him down.

The light of evening lay ahead.

In the light stood two soldiers with bared arms and bloody swords—and beyond the soldiers the bodies of mangled men.

The executioners lunged at him.

"Not this one!" shouted the revelers, running to his help. "This

man is acquitted. He is a friend of the Revolution. A hero!"

But they were too late. One of the murderers had aimed at his head with the flat of his sword.

"Stop, citizens!" yelled the revelers. "The Englishman is acquitted!"

They picked him up and carried him out of the terrible courtyard—and set him down in the street.

"We will get you help, citizen," said one of them, trying to stanch his wound.

"Take him to a surgeon," shouted another.

A *fiacre* had just drawn up on the opposite side. A face—the sharp, intelligent face he had seen watching him in the courtroom, looked out of the carriage window.

"I will take care of him, citizens," said an educated voice.

8

England

Once bundled into the *fiacre,* he must have fainted, for he came to himself in a house, in darkness—thick blood in his eyes—with two voices quite close to him, speaking so quickly to each other that he could not catch what they said. Then, iron hands pressed on his arms and chest, holding him down, and, with cool fingers probing his throbbing wound, he felt a fierce scraping and pricking of his torn flesh.

He must have fainted again, for he awakened to a new darkness.

"The surgeon says that the wound is serious, *mon ami,*" said the educated voice that had hailed him from the *fiacre.* "It is not dangerously deep, you must understand, but it is very close to your right eye."

He must stay here in Paris, he was told, with his head bandaged and his eyes covered till the surgeon came to him again.

"But why may I not see?" he protested.

"It is to protect your sight."

"And what am I to do? I have no friends," he had burst out, remembering bitterly how John Taverner had left him to his fate in the Place Vendôme—had fled in panic wearing his Camberstock coat.

"You are my guest, citizen. It is the least that France can do."

He must rest now, he was told; he must stay in bed; the maid would bring him a *tisane.* And, when he was feeling better, they must talk.

Three days later they did indeed talk.

His host's voice came to him out of the darkness—like a voice speaking inside his own head.

"You are a citizen, *mon ami,* not of France nor of England—but of the world!"

His own words!

"You are a friend of the Revolution!"

He had just declared it in open court.

"You are a friend of France."

He had just sworn this, too.

"We need allies, *mon ami.* France needs allies. Its enemies are gathered to destroy it."

This, too, he knew to be true.

"You must return to England, my hero," his host whispered hoarsely out of the darkness. "You must go among the young there, and the poor, and the disaffected, urging them to join us."

He felt his heart nearly breaking with despair. What else had he been doing all these many years?

He pleaded a fever and faintness—and the voice stopped.

But his host came to him the next day, and the day after, and the day after that.

"But I am *English,*" he protested. "If our two countries should go to war . . ."

"Freedom knows no frontiers, my friend."

How often had he declaimed this in the Debating Club at Oxford!

"There is much oppression in your country," the voice continued. "Yes, even in the England that our Voltaire once so much admired. You know it for yourself. Your cottagers are dispossessed of their commons; in the cities, your poor work like slaves in the rich men's mills. In high places, there is craft and corruption . . ."

It was true. All true.

And then, for a week, he must have been desperately ill. His head burned like fire; his whole body was wracked with pain. If he slept at all, then he woke with a scream, having heard again the howls of the men being done to death in that terrible prison yard. Visions of the slaughtered Swiss Guard and the wretched wagoner on his hurdle and the bodies of the prisoners lying in their own blood scorched the darkness under his bandages.

A woman sponged him with a cool cloth. He felt the softness of her fingers.

Then, he was weak but better again.

And the voices returned. There were two of them now. And the new one was harsh and incisive.

"We have saved you from death, citizen," his host began quietly. "We want little in return."

"You have but to do what you have done before," said the stranger sharply. "But to do it secretly, this time, and report your success to our agents."

Agents?

"Why, yes. Have you not guessed?" the stranger laughed. "We have agents throughout your country—men dedicated to freedom, like yourself, citizen."

It was all settled, they said, leaving him at last. When he was well enough to travel, they would give him money and a pass to the coast.

A month later, Stephen stood on the deck of the Channel packet boat watching the cliffs of Dover growing ever more distinct. Now they had put on whiteness; now they were lipped with grass; now they had samphire growing halfway down. He stood there, with his hat in his hand, letting the breeze cool the livid scar on his forehead, looking heartsick at the nearing beauty of England—and longing to be healed. The vessel glided into the harbor, its sails momentarily flapping as they lost the wind, and then nosed silently towards the wharf. Seagulls were screaming. Kentish voices were shouting along the quay.

" 'Ere's a young gentleman, Bill, what's got a fine clout on 'is 'ead," shouted a deckhand, laughing to a friend below him on shore.

Stephen, as he stumbled down the gangplank, thought the

fellow mocked him. He was no gentleman. He had no coat; no luggage; no pride—and only the Frenchman's money.

The man at the foot of the plank gave him a hand.

"They're a peevish set o' mucks t'other side," he said, smiling cheerfully. "But you're 'ome now, mate."

He tried to smile back. The warm bluntness of the English caught at his throat.

But home?

What was home?

He wandered away from the harbor in an anguished daze, heading northwards—as it happened—towards the Downs, but hardly knowing that it was north or that hills lay ahead. He was aware only that he was out of France. Out of France—but weighed down by that country's curse in his pocket. He saw a hedge with blackberries hanging in it, and above the blackberries a festoon of hops and the browning leaves of the hawthorn. And he stood a long time staring at this tangled autumn growth, seeing that it was beautiful and longing for its beauty to awake him from the nightmare that was traveling with him inside his head. He trudged on at last, knowing that the sun was shining, that the birds were singing, that the last apples were hanging golden in the orchards on either side of the road, that it was October, that this was Kent, the garden of England—but aware, too, that this peaceful world was cut off from him. It was as though he were imprisoned in a dark room, peering out at it through a pane of glass.

Later, on passing an oast-house and coming to a village, he saw that it was evening. Feeling even iller than he felt before, he wondered whether his trouble might not be hunger. There was an inn straight ahead of him—a simple place with a badly painted Duke of Marlborough swinging in its sign and a bench and a trestle outside.

He walked into the bar and asked for bread and cheese and a flagon of ale; at least, he *thought* he asked for it, but the voice making his demand did not seem to come out of his own mouth, but from another's. He looked round in surprise; but there was no one there who could have spoken. Two farm laborers were playing dominoes in a corner. By the fire sat an old man, heating a poker to put in his beer. Not one of them looked up.

"Going far?" the woman asked him, handing him his supper.

"No," he answered promptly.

No?

Why in Hell had he said "no"? He sat on the bench outside, staring at the rampant symmetry of a hop field, and wondered if he were going mad. He was not staying here in Kent. He was not staying anywhere. He had nowhere to stay.

As he sat there, gazing at the hop bines, he clutched at the haven of madness.

That was it! He was mad!

A madman had no past. No present. No future. A madman had no huge hopes for the world. No dishonor.

Why had he taken their damned money and their pass? Through weakness? Through fear? Through muddled thinking?

God knew!

He made up his mind again, as he stared at the graying hop field, that he had done what he had done—because he was mad.

Yet, if he were not truly mad, he was very near it.

Whether it was his wound or the sights in the prison or his vanished hopes, his mind seemed curiously out of balance and unlike itself. He could not control the way it worked. Having trudged north from Dover all afternoon, haunted by the horror of what he had done, he left the inn bench and walked on through the dusk till he came to a beech copse at the top of a hill. There, he sat down. And thought of Martha.

He had long ago forgiven Martha her insensitiveness to poetry. She was by nature earthbound, unmovable. He saw that now—and saw that this stolidness was a virtue in women. A man could find peace in such a girl. Forgetfulness. An end to grief. Hunched up against the night cold, he stared over the Downs and longed with his whole heart for what could never be: that he should drown himself in Martha—and never wake up. It was a

vain dream. For what could he offer her in return for such oblivion? A home? A profession? An untarnished loyalty to their
country?

He hated himself. He was useless. What good had he ever been
to anyone—at any time in his life? To Catherine? To Josh? To
Tristram Walkinshaw? To that canting coward—John Taverner? He had been a cross to them all. A curse to everyone
he had met. And why had he been branded with this mark of
Cain? Because of his devotion to freedom—a freedom he had just
seen dying in murder.

Starting to his feet in horror, he ran headlong down the hill
in the darkness. He had the price of that murder in his pocket!

He ran on and on, as though pursued by the Devil, down a
rutted lane, past a field of cabbages, over a stile towards a small
farm.

And there, at last, lay his salvation: a thick-mantled pond.

He stared at its dark scum, entranced. Then, in frenzied haste,
he felt in his pockets and pulled out every hateful English guinea
piece they had given him in Paris, and threw them in a shower
into the middle of the duckweed. He watched them glimmer
a moment and then sink—down, down into Kent's primeval
mud.

A week—ten days—he did not know—he wandered penniless
through Kent, grabbing berries out of the hedges, stealing apples,
sleeping in dry ditches or by haystacks, drinking water out of the
cattle troughs, conscious only that the sun was shining or that
it rained, that there was starshine or moonlight or mist; and that
the visible world was growing hourly more terrible to him. In a
hillside coppice he came upon a stoat and a crow and a jay crucified upon a railing in a "gamekeeper's larder"; he heard rabbits
screaming in snares—where no snares were.

At last, one day, he ran to free a live man hanging from a
gibbet in the middle of a field.

"Dear God! I am quite crazy," he cried, as he flung down the
scarecrow.

Greatly shaken by his plight, he tried to make his way to a turnpike.

That evening, sitting on its grass verge, he stared at a milestone. "London. Twenty miles," he read.

London! he thought with the last flicker of reasoning left to him. In London lay help. The East India Company. His Uncle Parkin's friends.

9

Catherine

On the same sunny October morning that Stephen stepped ashore at Dover, Catherine stopped on her way down the stairs at Town End—as she so often did—and looked out across the garden at Camberstock Hill. What she saw filled her with joy, which was odd, seeing how familiar it was to her. Yet it was always so. Each time she caught sight of the trees in the valley and the bald knob of the hill sticking up into the sky, they gave her a strange glow of pleasure. They did for her what Josh said a swig of rum did for him: they put heart into her—made her able to stomach, at least for a brief hour, the tedium and emptiness of her life in her uncles' house.

She had special need for some comfort today, for Josh, home after two years for ten days' leave, had set off for Garthdale last night alone. It was strange, but neither Josh nor Martha had invited her to accompany him. She felt piqued; and she felt lonely. He was to leave Garthdale on Saturday and travel straight down to London. She would not see him again.

She not only stopped on the stairs; she sat down on the windowsill and gave herself up to the view. Just below the craggy flank of the hill, sheep were cropping between the patches of russet bracken where the turf stretched, short and springy to one's feet. Farther down, a shaft of sunlight was falling on a gentle slope of mossy grass, splashing it a silvery gold. She held her breath. She had forgotten this slope till now. It was the "rolling slope"—the famous "rolling slope." Stephen and Josh and she used to roll down that slope in their childhood—faces wet with dew, the sky chasing the grass and the mints and the mosses, blue, then green; green, then blue, over and over, till the reedy tussocks at the bottom brought one to rest in the bog.

As she sighed for times past, she heard the mailboy's horn.

A letter for Town End!

She could see the boy's head bobbing up and down over the top of the stone wall.

Something for Uncle Fletcher? For Aunt Biddy? Or just the *Farmer's News* for Uncle Matthew? It did not matter what. Even a bill for coal would bring a little life into this sodden place.

"Who's it for?" she shouted, running across the spongy lawn.

"For Miss Parkin," shouted back the boy. "And all the way from London."

They met at the gate.

"Give it to me," she cried impatiently.

It must be from Stephen—from Stephen, at last.

But the boy, whom she had known all her life, held it firmly behind his back, teasing.

"It's a love letter," he grinned, knowingly. "Miss Parkin's got a sweetheart!"

"No, I haven't. No, I haven't," she flushed angrily. "Give it to me at once. It's from one of my brothers."

The boy handed it to her, reluctantly.

"Don't know why anyone should get so excited about a *brother*," he threw back at her as he went on his way.

But it was not from Stephen. The address was written in a handwriting that she had never seen before.

She tore it open.

It was from John Taverner.

As she read what he had to say, she felt cold. "He was arrested in the Paris streets . . . they threw him into prison . . . they would not tell me where." She felt the freezing clutch of fear. "Terrible things happened that weekend in the city . . . prisoners massacred . . . without trial. I have been everywhere . . . asked every official . . ."

As she sat in the carrier's cart, lurching across the moor towards Garthdale, the huge mountainside of her grief began moving.

The Paris prisons!

"Are you all right, miss?" asked the carrier.

She looked at him blankly and then nodded.

She had read about the massacres in the Paris prisons. They had sickened her—but not filled her with terror. Their horror had belonged to another world. And Stephen had been there! *Stephen!* Her brother! She shuddered. The accounts of brutal butchery in every prison in the city came back to her with an appalling stab of pain.

"It's only three miles more, miss," said the carrier. "We'll soon be at Garthdale."

Stephen had been so neglectful of her that she had not known he was in France. They had all thought that he was in London, seeking employment as a tutor.

And instead, he had been in Paris . . . through all those dreadful days!

Josh and Martha were as stunned by John Taverner's news as she. They stood staring, white-faced, at the letter—strangely together in their grief.

"Last d-day of August he was arrested," Josh burst out at last. "And t-today it's—"

"The fourth of October," Martha whispered.

Not one of them spoke. Nearly five weeks . . . and not a word. Stephen must surely be dead.

And then, in a fever of anguish, Catherine snatched back the letter and read it anew.

"What kind of friend is this John Taverner?" she cried out. "Why did he not *stay* with him when he was arrested? Why did he not go with him to the magistrate . . . to the prison?"

Martha shook her head. She had clutched Josh's hand.

None of them knew, stammered Josh . . . knew what things were like in Paris.

"Why does he not come to us himself?" Catherine went on. "Tell us *himself* how it was?"

Then, for the first time, she read the postscript.

"He is sending us Stephen's belongings by carrier!" she burst out. "By *carrier,* Josh—as though they were a bundle . . . a bundle of *anybody's* old clothes!"

At last her tears came to her. They rolled down her cheeks without ceasing.

They drove back to Town End, the three of them, in the stunned silence of grief.

Catherine perceived dully that something must have happened between Josh and Martha. They had come to an understanding. Were engaged, perhaps? She did not ask. She was too full of Stephen.

When they reached Camberstock, they found that the red-spotted bundle had already arrived.

Catherine took it upstairs quickly, out of the sight of her uncles, and undid it on her bed.

His threadbare, second-best coat; a razor; a pair of stockings that she had knitted; a shirt that she had made for him; and a battered little volume of poetry.

She stared at the things laid out on the counterpane in anguished disbelief. Could Stephen really be dead? Was this all that was left of a person so passionately devoted to life? All his anger and gaiety and rebelliousness came back to her in a rush—and her love for him. Through all the years of exasperation, she had loved him, she knew, far more deeply than she had ever loved Josh.

She turned from the bed and saw that Martha and Josh were standing behind her, staring too at Stephen's pathetic belongings.

"How s-strange that he should have t-taken this," said Josh, picking up the small volume and turning over its title page.

It was a close-print edition of *Paradise Lost*.

Martha was fingering the all-too-familiar threadbare coat.

"He must have had it cleaned," she said absently. "There used to be an ink stain on the sleeve."

Cleaned? Stephen have something *cleaned?*

"Yes!" exclaimed Catherine in astonishment. "And there's a new darn in the elbow!"

The two girls stood with the pitiful garment held between them, conjuring up strange secrets in Stephen's life that neither of them had ever suspected.

Two days later, Josh took the coach to London, and Martha returned to Garthdale.

It was a terrible time for Catherine, for she had to fight for

Stephen even in death. Her Uncle Matthew told her that it was a stupid way for an Englishman to have lost his life—getting himself mixed up with a mob of heathen foreigners.

Her Uncle Fletcher was even more cruel.

Courageous and self-contained though she tried to be, she nevertheless broke down one night at supper when the talk turned on a certain young neighbor who was going up to Oxford for the first time next term.

"Pull yourself together, Catherine," her uncle rasped impatiently. "Be thankful that your brother's death has spared you much grief!"

"Spared me much grief?"

"Would you have wanted a traitor for a brother? A man loyal, not to his King, but to those wicked revolutionaries in France?"

"But we aren't at war, yet!" she burst out in a flood of angry tears. "And when we are . . . you don't know how Stephen will feel!"

Her unconscious lapse into the future tense—her buried disbelief that Stephen was really dead—suddenly gave her back her courage.

"It's not *fair* of you!" she rounded on him. "Not fair to condemn him for something that may never be!"

He shrugged his shoulders. "The young man was unusually consistent in his folly," he said, returning unmoved to his lamb chop.

Yet, in this unfeeling household, she found one surprising champion of her brother.

Aunt Biddy.

Aunt Biddy was a poor, frightened goose of a woman. A fool. Stephen and she had agreed upon this years ago. But the goose had a tender heart.

The morning after her outburst at supper, she and Aunt Biddy were taking the children for an airing along the lane towards the lake. The sun was shining. The trees on the farther shore of Ullswater were aglow with their autumn gold.

"Your poor brother," sighed his aunt. "He used to love this time of year so much!"

So he had.

Now that Catherine came to think of it, the early autumn had always brought Stephen a gay kind of peace. He had smiled on them all on days like this—made plans for picnics and nutting and climbing the peaks. How strange of Aunt Biddy to have remembered! She walked on beside her towards the water, her heart warming towards her aunt.

"Catherine, my dear," she continued after a long pause. "It grieves me sorely that he was not happy with us . . . that he and his uncles could not agree . . ."

What could she say?

"He . . . he never understood how it was with my poor Fletcher."

How was it? she wondered grimly.

Her husband had had many cares, Aunt Biddy went on. He had had his good name to keep with the Duke—not only for himself but for all their sakes. He was the Duke's agent. His adviser. And Stephen's wildness had plagued him beyond bearing. Had made him ill.

Ill?

"Yes, my dear," she said timidly. "A wife always knows."

She spoke then of sleepless nights and of an irritability so intense that it had soured his temper and given him a pain in his side. And the pain—the recurring pain whenever Stephen's behavior was forced upon his attention—had made his harshness to them all a settled habit: a kind of protection against further pain.

"He was not always like this," she said sadly. "He was not ungentle—before the three of you came to us."

Catherine walked on full of anguish now that the past had been revealed to her in this new light.

"And now the poor boy is dead," said Aunt Biddy, a tear rolling down her pale cheek. "And it can never be put right between them!"

Catherine stooped to pick up Isaac, who had fallen in the mud. When she had cleaned him up, she set him on his way again, laughing to himself.

"If Stephen really *is* dead," she said quietly to her aunt, "then things should be put right to his memory."

After this, she showed a warmer understanding in her attentions to Aunt Biddy and made a still sterner resolve never to break down on Stephen's account in front of her Uncle Fletcher. Stephen and her grief for him were to be kept for herself alone. Both were too precious to be wrangled over in public. In the privacy of her bedroom, however, she spent bitter nights and awoke each morning to a more urgent consciousness of her grievous loss, for every night and day that passed without news of her brother made it the more certain that he was dead.

It was Stephen himself whom she mourned most; but she had leisure and loneliness enough in which to contemplate her own unhappy plight. It had been Stephen who was to take her away from this loveless house, Stephen who was to offer her a home, Stephen who was to introduce her to books, ideas, young friends —and to an eager purpose in life. And, in return, it had been upon Stephen that she was to bestow the sisterly devotion and love that filled her heart.

What was to become of her now?

She knew herself to be naïve and ignorant and inexperienced in the ways of the world. But she was not a fool. Marriage was, now, her only hope of escape from Town End. But it was unlikely that she would marry. She had no dowry. And she was not handsome—as Martha was handsome. The face that looked back at her out of Aunt Biddy's mirror was bright-eyed and healthy. That was all. She was too poor a match for the sons of the local gentry, and the retired manner in which she lived in her uncles' house made it impossible for her to have a wider acquaintance. Martha's home at Garthdale was the farthest she had ever strayed. Living so buried from the world—without money or goods looks—how was she ever to meet a man whom she could love or, indeed, one who might love her in return? She wept for her brother's death. And she wept for herself. Without Stephen, she was stuck here forever.

Live with Josh and Martha? She looked at the idea—and then frowned and let it pass. They were too newly in love, and their future too vague. Besides, Josh—shot up to a man, and a brusque and silent one at that—was almost a stranger to her. He had been too long away—and had traveled too far.

And Martha?

She winced. Martha's hand clutching Josh's as they read the letter together that morning at Garthdale had given her an intolerable jab of pain—for Stephen.

Poor Stephen, she wept again. Even if he were alive, what would he come back to? Not to Martha.

And then, a week later, when life and hope seemed at their lowest ebb—with a harsh toot on the mailboy's horn—came the letter from Josh.

This is what he wrote:

> 12th October
> *Earl of Cape Wrath*
> off Gravesend

Dearest Catherine,

Stephen is not dead. He is here on board with us. He is ill. In rags. He knows me. Knows Uncle Parkin. But little else. We are giving him money and food and clothes, but we are at our wits' end. We sail in the morning. We must catch the wind. He asks for you and Martha. We told him that he should go to Town End but he shook his head. Then I said "Ellenhead"; and he seemed to agree. He came to us last evening, sent downriver by kind order of Mr. Saville, a director of the Company. And we are sending him back to Mr. Saville with instructions that he be put on the coach for Ellenhead. Pray God Mr. Walkinshaw will receive him. Please go to him immediately. And please write me by express to the Cape to tell me he is safe.

> In haste, your loving brother, Josh.

She ran to Aunt Biddy with Josh's letter and they clasped each other and wept in pure joy, with the two children tugging at their skirts, crying to know what was up.

"Stephen's alive," she shouted, swooping down and lifting Isaac up to her. "Stephen's not dead, Isaac. He's *alive!*"

" 'Tephen?" lisped the puzzled child.

"I must go, Aunt Biddy," she burst out. "Must go at once to Ellenhead."

"To Ellenhead? To Mr. Walkinshaw's? But, my dear, someone must go with you."

"Someone go *with* me?" she gasped, suddenly pale, seeing herself sitting beside Uncle Fletcher in the cart all the way over the Kirkstone Pass.

"Yes. We must send for Martha."

"For Martha?"

Her happiness had driven out her wits.

"He is a bachelor, Catherine. And he has no housekeeper."

"Mr. Walkinshaw?" she exclaimed, laughing. "But Aunt Biddy, he's an old man. And Stephen . . . Stephen'll be there!"

Being able to say his name again—openly and in joy—filled her with such an intensity of happiness that she whirled the child in her arms so quickly through the air that he began to cry.

Martha? she thought, through the child's howls. She did not want Martha to go with her.

"But, Aunt Biddy!" she expostulated, putting the boy down. "I can't wait for Martha to be got from Garthdale. I really can't. Look, Josh says: 'Go to him *immediately.*' Stephen needs me. I must go to him *now*."

But, for almost the first time in her life, poor, goose-witted Aunt Biddy stood firm. Stephen might not have arrived yet in Ellenhead, she said. And it was clear that when he did, Catherine would have to stay with him and nurse him.

"He sounds very ill, my dear. Martha will be a help to you."

"I can look after him myself. I'm his *sister,* Aunt Biddy."

"All the same, dear," said the obstinate woman, "Martha must go with you. It'll . . . it'll set Mr. Walkinshaw's mind at rest."

10

Ellenhead

Two days later, Catherine and Martha came to Ellenhead. The school and the schoolmaster's house lay at the back of the church, they were told. And, on rounding the corner by the lych gate, they saw him: saw Stephen, sitting on a log with his back to them in a small, low-walled garden.

Catherine wanted to shout out her joy and run to him; but Martha held her back.

"No, don't," she urged in a low voice. "You may frighten him. Let's come to him quietly."

He was wearing an old naval coat with the collar pulled up about his ears. His elbows were propped up on his knees, his head clasped in his hands, and his eyes fixed on the ground. That's the way he sits when he's thinking something out, was the thought that darted through Catherine's mind. But as they approached, she thought: No. Not like that. When he's struggling with an idea, he shrugs his shoulders, or shakes his head, or clutches at the grass, or snaps a twig! He did not move a muscle all the time that they were approaching him along the lane—and this was odd, for the cold autumn wind was blowing his hair about. The garden gate shrieked on its rusty hinge, but he still did not look up. Even as they walked towards him over the lawn, he did not stir. She wondered whether he were fast asleep, sitting up.

As they tiptoed across the grass, she was aware that someone had come out of the schoolmaster's house and was standing behind them—but she could not take her eyes off Stephen. He

looked so ill and unlike himself. Shipwrecked, somehow. Abandoned.

Martha, putting her finger to her lips, motioned Catherine to stay where she was; then, gliding round the edge of the log, she came up behind him, stooped down, and with both hands gently lifted up his bowed head.

Catherine cried out.

A livid gash on his forehead made him look maimed. He looked at her, at first not recognizing her, out of hot, sunken eyes.

"Catherine," he sighed at last.

She ran to him, knelt down, and took him in her arms, and he dropped his head on her shoulder, rolling it slightly from side to side. His forehead felt dreadfully hot.

"He's ill," she whispered, looking up through his blown hair at Martha, stooping over them both.

He had stopped rolling his head. He seemed suddenly fast asleep.

Martha came quietly round to the front of the log, saw the terrible scar, and then stooped down and put her hand on his flushed cheek.

"He has a fever," she whispered. "We must get him to bed."

"Stephen," said Catherine aloud, trying to rouse him. "We think that you are ill—that you should go indoors—go to bed."

And then, something horrible happened. He raised his head, shuddering all over. His face was contorted with fear.

"Not *indoors!*" he cried out. "Not in *bed!* Don't . . . don't shut me up."

He had got to his feet, shaking them off.

"Stephen," said a man's voice. "We are friends. No one is going to shut you up."

Catherine looked quickly over her shoulder. A tall man. Stephen's schoolmaster. He would know what to do. He would help them. He would rouse them all from this nightmare.

"And no one is going to put you to bed," he went on. "Not against your will."

Mr. Walkinshaw's familiar voice must have reassured him. He grew calmer.

"But it's cold out here," said Catherine, her teeth beginning to chatter. "Let's all go into the house."

Then, the horrible thing happened again. Her brother turned wildly upon her and then, as suddenly, darted away as though he did not trust her. He was shivering again. He was back in his terror.

"No. No," he cried out hoarsely. "It's safer. Much *safer* in the garden."

She was appalled. It came to her that Stephen was quite mad. She turned desperately to the tall stranger and found him looking this way and that about his small garden and running his hand through his iron-gray hair. Looking at him, she felt better. Mr. Walkinshaw was clearly not alarmed. He was merely wracking his brains.

"A bonfire!" he exclaimed at last. "We'll make a bonfire! That's what we'll do!"

She looked at him in amazement.

"Miss Penrose," he said quickly. "You'll find wood shavings in that shed over there. Miss Parkin, there are fallen twigs under the apple trees. I'll go and see what I can find in the house."

If this was some sort of game, she thought bewilderedly, then they had better try to play it.

"And, Stephen," called out the schoolmaster from a downstairs window. "Don't stand about getting cold. Pull the dead bindweed out of the hedge."

Ten minutes later there was a bonfire roaring in the little garden such as she had only seen before on Guy Fawkes' Night. A box of unbound sermons, a worn-out laundry basket, and a worm-eaten chair without a seat were blazing away in the raw October wind. The cold autumn air shimmered with heat, and in the shimmers floated fragile petals of gray ash as soft as moth wings. She sat and watched them, entranced. Then, looking across at Stephen sitting quietly on the grass beside Martha, she saw at once the virtue of the fire. He was staring into the embers, his whole being absorbed in its glowing depth. His terror had gone. He had forgotten his nightmare world. The lines in his cheeks were uncreasing. He was growing drowsy. As she watched, he suddenly crumpled up and, putting his head in Martha's lap, was asleep.

With Stephen at last at peace, she looked about her. Mr. Walkinshaw had left them. He must have gone back into the house.

She followed him quietly and found him sitting in a bare, uncomfortable little study to the right of the front door. His head was cupped in his hands.

She sat down opposite him and felt the tears crawling down her cheeks. Stephen, whom she had thought dead, was alive—but destroyed.

Mr. Walkinshaw looked up.

"You must not cry," he said gently.

"No. I mustn't," she gulped, feeling in her sleeve and her bodice for her pocket handkerchief.

"It won't help him, Catherine," he said sadly, passing her his own.

In the midst of her grief it shot through her that this schoolmaster was too young to treat her as a child.

"No. It won't," she agreed.

And then the full weight of her fear fell upon her.

"Stephen's mad, isn't he?" she burst out, longing to unload her burden onto this man.

He did not reply for a moment, but sat looking at her attentively, as though sizing her up.

"What do you mean when you say someone is mad?" he asked gravely.

"But Stephen is *different*. You know he is!"

He nodded.

"Something terrible has happened to him," he replied. "But . . . but I don't know what."

They wondered together how he had come by such a wound.

"Yet, it is not just his physical condition," said the schoolmaster. "It is his terror. He must have seen dreadful things."

"In the prison," she shuddered. "It must have been there."

"Prison? What prison?"

"Don't you know?"

As she stared across at him in astonishment, she suddenly realized that if Stephen had not told him himself, Mr. Walkinshaw might very well not have heard of his visit to Paris and his arrest. She told him quickly what John Taverner had written in his letter.

"Stephen in prison during the Paris massacres!" he exclaimed in horror, suddenly white in the face.

He leaped to his feet and strode to the window. Catherine joined him. Together, they stood staring out at him asleep by the bonfire in Martha's lap.

"No wonder he has such terrible dreams! No wonder he can't bear being shut up in the house!"

He described to her the anguished night he had just spent with Stephen. He had kept nodding off and then suddenly starting up with a cry, shivering and sweating with terror. Just before dawn, he had fallen into a deeper and more tranquil sleep, but when the Ellenhead church bells began ringing at eight o'clock, he had leaped out of bed with a terrible shout and had run out into the garden in his nightshirt.

"Just think, Catherine," said Mr. Walkinshaw in puzzled sadness. "Church bells! English church bells! Can you imagine a more peaceful sound? Yet, they filled him with terror."

She shook her head. She could not understand it at all. Stephen had always loved the sound of church bells. Go to church he would not. But to hear the bells ringing out down the valleys had filled him with pleasure.

"They are the poor man's music, Catherine," he had told her once.

As they stood looking at him, baffled by the terrible state he was in, they watched Martha slowly hook an armful of straw towards her from the bale that Mr. Walkinshaw had brought out from his shed. She made it into a rough pillow and gently lowered Stephen's head onto it. Then she got up, stooped down to stir the bonfire, stood up, shook out her skirt, and walked towards them.

"He's ill. *Physically* ill," she told them. He had a fever. His skin felt burning hot. Besides, he was starved. It was clear that he had not eaten properly for weeks.

"We must call a doctor," she said.

Mr. Walkinshaw, to their surprise, shook his head.

"I suggested that to him last night," he said. "It drove him into one of his panics."

"A *doctor*?" she burst out. "Why?"

The schoolmaster looked at her in grave concern.

"Catherine, it is not only you who fear your brother may be mad. He fears it himself. A doctor means only one thing to him: an order for a committal to Bedlam."

"But, he's *not* mad!" said Martha forthrightly. "He's crazed with lack of sleep. He's overwrought. He's ill with fever. Isn't there a doctor here whom Stephen *knows?* Whom he can trust?"

Their host again shook his head.

"There's a new man at Ellenhead now. Old Dr. Hyslop, who used to look after the school while Stephen was there, has retired."

"Where does he live?"

"Ten miles away. Over at Ambleside."

"Let's fetch him."

After a night made terrible to him, not by the prisoners' cries but by the two voices tempting him in the darkness, Stephen awoke in a trembling sweat to find Martha, with a lighted candle in her hand, dressed in her nightshift, bending over him.

"Out of Hell, I've come to Heaven," he thought hopefully, holding his breath.

"Catherine's gone to heat you up some milk," said the heavenly apparition, shivering a little with cold as she put down the candle in order to plump up his pillows. "After a hot drink, you must try to start the night afresh."

"Where am I?" he sighed happily.

"At Ellenhead, of course. Catherine and I are here to look after you until you are better."

"I'm ill?"

"You've got a fever. Dr. Hyslop's coming in the morning to give you a prescription for it."

It all sounded so normal and commonplace, said in Martha's casual tone of voice. Like a bad cold in the head.

"Old Snuff-face?" he asked dreamily.

"Snuff-face? Yes, that's who."

When he awoke again, he was conscious that the old fool must have been in the room for quite some time. He could hear his voice talking. But he could not be bothered to turn over in bed and look at him. He felt pleasantly disembodied. Perhaps the old idiot had already given him one of his noxious drafts.

"Just a malignant fever," Old Snuff-face was summing up. "A

great perturbation of spirits and a long-standing want of proper victuals."

He lay there on the farther shore of life, listening to the old doctor grumbling loudly as he walked down the stairs.

"God knows what young men are doing to themselves these days," he said. "There's young Fanshawe over at Bracerigg just killed himself with opium, Lord Norland's heir drinking himself to death, and now this young gentleman upstairs, poking his nose in French affairs and getting his head knocked in for his pains. Why cannot they behave as the Almighty meant them to behave?"

"And how's that?" asked Martha's amused voice.

"Stay at home, young lady. Stay at home. Look after their estates. Eat good English beef. Drink ale."

Catherine rejoiced in Dr. Hyslop's verdict.

But they still had far to go.

As her brother's fever slowly left him, she watched him sink into a dreadful lethargy. He did not read; he did not talk; he did not even look out of the window at the scurrying October clouds. He seemed lost within himself.

"I'm a great nuisance to you all," he said wretchedly when they brought him food; and, having eaten, he turned his face again to the wall.

Not even a rick catching fire on the hill above the village summoned him back to life.

"It's so unlike him," she said wretchedly one evening, as she sat in the study below, darning Mr. Walkinshaw's socks. "Stephen used to be so interested in everything that went on."

"Even when it made him angry," replied his schoolmaster with a wry smile.

She looked up quickly, made sharply aware yet once again of Mr. Walkinshaw's swift understanding. It was true. It was Stephen's *anger* that she missed.

She looked again secretly at this man who understood her brother so well. He was reading his pupils' themes. He was not very old; not more than thirty-six, at a rough guess, though his graying hair and the muddle he lived in made him appear at first sight to be more. A smile of amusement was playing round his lips as he corrected the boys' work.

She turned her attention again to his sock and found that the hole in it was grinning up at her—as though they had just shared a joke.

No wonder Josh had liked him, too, she thought, as she re-threaded her needle. He was so clearly a kind man. A tolerant man. A man to be repected. No. Respect was not enough. He deserved better than that. Her heart warmed to him as she considered him. Mr. Walkinshaw was the only grown-up she had ever met who had spoken of Stephen with affection. *Real* affection. And *pride*.

"Catherine," he had said that first night. "Stephen is the finest pupil I have ever had here at Ellenhead. We must cherish him between us. We must get him well again. He has a great future ahead of him."

"What kind of future?" she had asked him, numb with despair.

"I don't know," he had admitted honestly. "But I am sure that there is something good and great that he has been born to do."

She stole a third look at him now, over the latticework of her darn—and suddenly felt her heart turning over inside her—in headlong joy.

Then she checked herself, frowning.

At the end of the second week, Stephen was making her anxious on a different count. He was coming painfully back to life, but the object of his journey seemed solely to be Martha.

He could not bear her out of his sight.

Catherine listened to Martha talking to him—telling him, as he begged, about her life at Garthdale, about the novels she read, about anything in which he showed an interest; and her heart ached for her brother, seeing yet more pain for him in the days ahead.

To do her justice, Martha was just as unhappy as she.

"No," she said to Stephen. "Let it be Catherine who reads to you this morning. Not me."

"Why not *you,* Martha?" he pleaded. "It's you I want."

The anguish of the situation became unbearable.

"Stephen," Catherine said to him, when they were alone. "Now that you are getting better, the two of us must go back to Town End."

"Town End!" he cried out. "Catherine, you can't mean it! I can't go back to Town End—*ever!"*

Seeing how ill he still looked and guessing how much he had suffered, and remembering her uncles' taunts, she did not think he really could.

But what could they do? Martha must go—for both Stephen's and her own sakes. But how *could* she go? Now that Catherine had lived here a fortnight in the schoolmaster's house, she had begun to see why Aunt Biddy's proprieties must be preserved. Not for her sake—but for his: for Mr. Walkinshaw's. He was the headmaster of a famous school. He was much respected in Ellenhead. He was a bachelor. He lived alone. He must not be made the object of slander or gossip on their account.

At last, Martha herself could bear it no longer.

"Catherine," she said. "I must either tell him or I must leave. It's not fair going on like this—not fair either to Stephen or to Josh or to myself."

"All right," she said grimly, knowing what it was that she must do. "But wait till tomorrow. I will speak to Mr. Walkinshaw tonight."

She did not know how to begin.

"Martha has got to go home," she blurted out.

He looked up in surprise from correcting a set of Greek verses. "Go home? She has not had bad news?"

"No. She's in love with Josh," she soldiered on painfully.

"With Joshua? Your brother?"

She nodded.

"Does he return her affections?" he asked, smiling with amusement. "Or is that a question I should not ask?"

Yes. The two had come to some sort of an understanding, she replied bleakly—during Josh's last leave.

"Lucky young woman," he replied briefly, returning to his correcting.

This was so little what she had expected that she went on sitting there, watching him, entirely nonplussed.

He looked up a minute later and must have caught the bafflement in her expression.

"Catherine, my dear!" he exclaimed in remorse. "I have been stupid. It is because of Stephen that she must leave?"

She nodded.

"He does not know about this understanding—and he is growing fond of the girl?"

She nodded again.

"Then your friend must go tomorrow," he said, jumping to his feet and scattering the Greek verses on the floor. "I will go and hire the carrier tonight. That's it. He can drive her over to Camberstock in the morning."

"But . . ." she stammered, growing scarlet in the face.

"But what?" he asked.

"Aunt Biddy . . . she says . . ."

She was so embarrassed that she could not go on.

"What does your Aunt Biddy say, Catherine, that causes you such distress?"

She closed her eyes and took a deep breath.

"That it isn't proper for me to stay in this house," she bolted out, "without . . . without another woman."

In the silence that followed she fancied she heard someone catching back a laugh.

"Do you think yourself, Catherine, that you will come to any harm?" he asked her, gravely enough.

"No," she replied honestly. "It's not *me,* Mr. Walkinshaw. It's *you* that Aunt Biddy's afraid for."

"Goodness me!" he exclaimed in amused astonishment. "I should not have thought you to be such a very dangerous young woman!"

"But, I'm not!" she burst out in extreme distress. "It's what your neighbors might think—she says."

He sat down beside her then and spoke to her gently. It was Stephen they both loved, he said. And Stephen needed them both. Martha must go at once—before his growing love for her caused him greater pain.

"He will get over it," he said calmly, "once she is out of the house."

"Do you think so?" she asked doubtfully.

Stephen was a man of many resources, he said. And of courage, too. When he was well enough to be told how matters stood, he would deal with his disappointment bravely enough.

"As for ourselves, dear Catherine," he said, taking her hand, "we can surely put up with a little slander to help your brother get well."

Next morning, Martha was off in the carrier's cart to Ambleside and Camberstock before Stephen was awake.

"It's better thus," she said to Catherine as they walked down the Ellenhead street.

When Catherine returned, she found Stephen wandering about the house, unshaven and distraught, in his nightshirt.

"Where has she gone?" he asked. "Where has Martha gone?"

"She's been called back to Garthdale," she said briefly, hating herself.

"Why? Is her father ill?"

"No. It's just that he wants her back. She's been here three weeks. It's a long time."

"But *I* want her, Catherine," he said brokenly.

"She is his daughter, Stephen," she said, feeling the tears rising in her eyes as she saw his shipwrecked condition.

"He's got his wife," he replied with a feeble flicker of the old anger.

"And you've got me," she answered with a brave smile. "Come, let me get hot water for your morning shave."

Three days later, Tristram Walkinshaw deemed it time to tell Stephen the truth. Indeed, it was becoming urgent that someone should, for Stephen was now sitting downstairs with them in the study, writing Martha what must surely be a love letter.

"Stephen," said their host gently. "Catherine and I both think that you should know how matters really stand."

"What matters, Tristram?" he asked, without looking up from his writing.

"About Martha."

"What about her?" he asked, swinging round to face him.

"She has plighted her troth to another."

Stephen seemed to have difficulty in understanding what was meant.

"Do you mean that Martha is in love with someone else?" he burst out at last.

"Yes."

"Is this true, Catherine?" he asked wretchedly.

She nodded.

"Who? Who is she in love with?"

Catherine looked up in misery and saw that Tristram Walkinshaw, standing behind her brother, was watching her with a tender concern.

"Stephen," she said gently. "Josh and Martha came to an understanding with each other during Josh's last leave."

"Josh?" he cried out. "Martha is in love with *Josh?*"

He looked wildly at them both—and then ran out of the room.

Darting to the window, they were in time to see him hurtling across the sodden winter garden and leaping over the low stone wall into the lane below.

"I must go after him," she cried, running to the study door.

But Tristram Walkinshaw was there before her.

"No, Catherine. You must *not* go."

"But he's in pain. He's ill. He's in despair."

She struggled fiercely; but he held her firm.

"Catherine, dear Catherine," he said tenderly, while she still pummeled him on the chest. "Don't you see you can't help him? No one can. He has got to live this through by himself."

After her storm of tears, he added sorrowfully: "Now, my dear, you have learned the saddest thing that anyone has to learn in life."

"What's that?" she hiccupped.

"That . . . that we can't really help those we love."

"Can't we?" she asked, feeling the sobs rising again in her throat.

"No," he said sadly, turning away from her and staring across his bedraggled garden in the direction that Stephen had fled. "They can only help themselves."

II

Pastures New

Stephen came to himself far up Ellen Glen, sitting on a stone and staring across the brook at a sheep.

All was gone now: his hopes for France; for mankind; for himself. Martha, his last refuge, loved Josh. Lowering his eyes in despair, he caught sight of the lingering threads of toadstools growing pallidly at his feet and smashed them with his boot.

For what reason had he been born? What had been the purpose of so much hope? He had wanted to help people—simple people. He had wanted to bring them freedom and happiness and a proper pride. *Where* had he gone wrong?

His whole headlong career passed before his eyes as he sat there staring at the smashed fungi: his protest four years ago in the Camberstock market square; the drubbing he had had in the inn yard; Catherine's tears; poor Josh going to sea; Oxford; St. Gilles; the mangled Swiss Guard; the prison . . . and there he stopped. For after the prison had come his terrible disgrace. The voices. The money. His wandering through Kent. He could not bear to think of what he had done. Yet, think he must. He must face it—accept it—for he had to live with it. For three nightmare weeks, he had been a traitor to his country. At the bottom of some Kentish duck pond lay the tokens of his guilt.

"Dear Heavens!" he groaned. "Let no man ever dredge them up!"

He raised his eyes from the ground and gazed in anguish at a mossy rock and at a bare rowan tree growing aslant the brook, and then again at the sheep, cropping the narrow patch of turf at the top of its precipitous crag—realizing with every familiar object that he saw that his treachery could not so easily be buried in the mud. He had betrayed that rock, that tree, that brook, that sheep. He had been disloyal to Tristram, to Catherine, to Martha, to Josh. In taking the Frenchman's bribe, he had murdered all that was good in himself.

He sighed in utter wretchedness.

Not even marrying Martha and living virtuously forever could have given him back his innocence. He saw that, now. She would not have brought him oblivion—only an incommunicable self-reproach.

He listened absently to the plaintive bleating of the sheep.

There was no escape, he despaired. He had to trail this hateful self about with him for the rest of his life.

And then the repeated cry of the sheep brought him back to the glen and to the crag across the brook.

He looked at the creature. It was an old, black-faced wether.

"Good God!" he cried, jumping to his feet. "It's trapped!"

He leaped across the brook to its aid. He must get the wether down off its precipitous perch before nightfall or it might tumble headlong into the brook and drown.

He had done it before—climbed up a rock and lifted a sheep down.

Could he do it now? He tried hard. He tried again and again, straining and sweating—but it was beyond him. He was still weak after so much illness.

Sobbing with a new frustration, he ran as fast as he could back to Ellenhead.

"Tristram," he shouted, bursting into Walkinshaw's study in the gloaming. "One of Crackenthorpe's wethers is stuck on a rock up the glen!"

Yet, though he had come back to the two of them waiting so anxiously in the dusk, though he had not thrown himself in the lake—as Catherine in her terror had feared he might—there was a long haul ahead for them all. She watched her brother through that dark November eat and sleep and put on flesh. But he did not grow happier. He seemed cut off from them both by a secret grief.

In the long, quiet days of his getting well, his grief was caused by the terrible tug-of-war still going on inside him. With the horrors of the massacre muted and veiled by his long illness, he found that he loved France still; still cherished the Revolution's hopes of a new Heaven upon earth. He remembered the joy of the villagers dancing under the trees; he heard again the strong voices of the young soldiers singing *La Marseillaise* as they marched through Breteuil in the dawn. And then, he felt his love of England: its ordinary people; its fields; its hills. And over the struggle of these warring loves, night and day, day and night, flapped the evil wings of his own guilt.

The struggle was a torment to him. And so was his remorse.

"Tell us what happened, Stephen," asked Tristram Walkinshaw at last.

The request, dropped so suddenly into the quiet room, startled him out of his abstraction.

What had happened? What, indeed!

He looked at them both. Tristram. Catherine. The two people he loved best in all the world. Tristram, tired out by his week's teaching. Catherine, bright-eyed and anxious, looking up from the piles of garments and curtains and tablecloths she had found to mend in this ragged house.

He began. And he went on. He told them everything.

When he had finished, the silence came back again. Catherine was weeping without a sound. Tristram looked suddenly old with sadness. He had tortured them with his story, he thought bleakly—and to no end.

But he was wrong.

"Stephen," said his friend, at last breaking the long silence. "You have suffered more than a man should be asked to suffer . . ."

He bowed his head.

"You should not blame yourself for what followed after . . ."

"Not *blame* myself?" he flung back bitterly.

"Many would have done much worse a thing."

What could be worse, he wondered, than to sell oneself to save one's life? His despair must have shown in his face.

"Come, Stephen, be sensible," said his former schoolmaster, quite sharply. "What harm have you done your country? None. You have sold no secrets. Betrayed no trust. Besides, man, England and France are not yet at war."

It was true. Perhaps it was not treason that he had committed. It was something else.

"Those Frenchmen of yours have cheated you of your self-esteem. That's all."

Catherine looked from one to the other—from the man that she loved to the brother that she loved—and heard not a word. She could not wrench her mind away from the terrible account of how Stephen had received the gash in his forehead; the horror of that prison yard was present with her in the quiet room.

"It is time that you put the past behind you," Tristram continued. "It is over, Stephen. Done with. You must think, now, what you are going to do with the rest of your life."

The rest of his life?

That night it stretched before his eyes as wide and as empty as a desert.

Just after Christmas the hard frosts set in, and Ellenmere froze firm from shore to shore. Catherine walked to the end of the town and gazed longingly at the field of ice, and wondered if she dared write to Aunt Biddy and ask her to send them both their skates.

She had hardly sat down in the study to pen this request when Tristram burst in, running his hands through his hair, and exclaiming in extreme exasperation:

"Well, that takes care of my assistant, damn it!"

"What's happened?" asked Stephen.

"The poor fool's fallen through the ice!"

"Good Heavens!" cried Catherine in distress. "Is Mr. Fordwick drowned?"

"No. No. Of course not. But he's broken his leg. I've no assistant next term for the Lower School."

And then swinging round, his gaze alighted upon his former pupil, lounging in a chair, reading Hume's *Treatise of Human Nature.*

". . . Unless . . . unless *you* take his place. That's it, Stephen, *you* be my assistant for eight weeks . . . till the leg is mended. You'll do splendidly. You're a much better scholar than poor Fordwick . . ."

"*I* teach the Lower School! But . . . but I would not be any good at it."

"Why not? You are just the man!"

Stephen, remembering his own wild insubordination in the Lower School, smiled wanly.

"Set a thief to catch a thief?" he asked. "Is that it?"

"If you like," replied Tristram laughing. "But, seriously, do you not see—it will give you time to consider carefully what you *really* want to do with your life."

"Oh, Stephen!" exclaimed Catherine excitedly. "Do say you'll do it. Please do! And I'll tell Aunt Biddy straight away that you are staying on here—and that I can't possibly return to Town End for at least another two months."

Then, suddenly realizing how transparent she had made her own longings, she turned her back on the room to hide her hot cheeks and went on writing her letter.

"Catherine," came Tristram's voice to her through her confusion. "What talk is this of your going back to Town End?"

"I've got to sometime," she replied shortly, without raising her head. "Aunt Biddy needs my help with the children."

"Not nearly so much as we poor bachelors need it here," he said soberly. "So, let us hear no more of your going."

To everyone's contentment, they heard no more—for weeks and weeks.

Stephen, meanwhile, plunged into his teaching.

It was a great solace to him being among the boys again—even though he sat so strangely on the other side of the master's desk; for the sound of them repeating their lessons and the shouts of them playing in the schoolyard had come over the wall to him, sitting idle and unhappy in the schoolmaster's house, reminding him achingly of times past—when he was young in hope. But, in charge now of thirty unformed and quite different minds—some eager, some cautious, most stuck deep in natural sloth—he had no time to contemplate the past, or France, or even himself.

"Dear Heaven!" he thought, worn out one evening at the end of his first fortnight as assistant. "What hard work it is to teach one poor, scrubbed little boy how to read!"

The trouble was that one could explain, encourage, cajole—but the wretched child had to do it *himself*. One could not do it for him.

Tristram, seeing his tiredness, gave him a wry smile.

"Yes, it's hard work when one comes down to it," he said. "Teaching a boy how to acquire even the first freedom exhausts the mind."

" 'The first freedom'?" he asked in surprise. "What do you mean?"

"Why, the freedom to read, of course. The freedom of books. Of great minds. Even the freedom to read *Romance of the Forest*," he ended, smiling as he looked at Catherine deep in Mrs. Radcliffe's novel.

The first freedom! Stephen took the thought to bed with him that night and looked at it this way and that. Then, he relinquished it, sighing a little as he did so. Tristram was wrong. Reading was not the first freedom. The first freedom for a man was to have enough to eat; the second was to think and speak and act as he saw fit. Only after these came reading. Then he sighed again. This life at Ellenhead was not for him. It was too easy. Too privileged. These boys, having rich parents, could somehow fumble into their reading—and their Greek and Latin, too—without his special intervention. His future lay elsewhere. In a harder, darker world.

Next evening, still pondering how he might come upon this world and what, indeed, was to be his task in bringing it light, he was surprised to be summoned peremptorily to a quite different concern.

Catherine had set out to walk down to Ellenhead to change her novel at the library. He and Tristram were correcting their school exercises in silence.

"Stephen," his friend barked out almost fiercely. "I have a favor to ask of you."

"You a favor to ask of *me?"* he exclaimed, astonished not only by the words but by the odd awkwardness in his voice.

"You are the head of your family," Tristram continued with a nervous, darting smile. "So it is you that I must ask."

He frowned. There was only one head of his family that he had ever heard of—and that was Uncle Fletcher.

"I want your permission to ask your sister for her hand in marriage."

He gaped at him, hardly believing his ears.

"You want to marry Catherine?" he exclaimed, in amazement.

"I am much too old for her, I know," his poor friend stumbled on in embarrassment. "I am thirty-six. She is only twenty. And . . . and I cannot offer her great wealth."

"Do you mean you *love* Catherine?" he burst out, in brotherly incomprehension.

"I have loved her from the moment I set eyes on her," he replied simply.

"And . . . and you want to . . . to *marry* her . . . and live with her for always?"

Tristram burst out laughing. His crisis was over.

"But of course, Stephen," he laughed again. "That's what marriage means!"

He was struck quite dumb. He could not understand it at all. He loved Catherine as a sister. She was cheerful and affectionate and loyal. But for Tristram's wife! Catherine would not be able to discuss Hume with Tristram, or Plato or Aristotle. She would bring nothing to the marriage. No money. Nothing.

Tristram must have mistaken his silence, for he went on in some distress:

"Stephen, I think she will come to love me in time. I . . . I would not ask her if . . . if . . . I did not think that she liked me a little already. I will be kind to her. I shall not be harsh."

"Tristram," he shouted joyfully. "Of course you can marry Catherine. I cannot think of a kinder, wiser, gentler husband for any girl to have!"

Later that night, when Tristram had asked his sister to marry him and she—with great happiness—had accepted him, the three sat round the table in the lamplight, making their plans. Stephen was to give her away; not Uncle Fletcher. On that they were all agreed. And the wedding was to be here at Ellenhead; not at Town End. Catherine could not bear the thought of her uncles playing any part in so joyful a day—though she felt a pang of regret for Aunt Biddy.

"But how soon can it be?" she asked eagerly.

"Well, it can't be tomorrow!" Tristram teased her.

There were such things as wedding clothes and marriage banns and the governors of the school to be told.

Stephen sat watching them both, still secretly surprised at his old friend's choice; but as he watched, he saw how brightly Catherine's eyes were shining and what a bloom of freshness lay on her cheeks. The lamplight shone a blessing on her youth— and a blessing, too, upon the snowdrops she had picked and put into a bowl on the table.

That's the explanation, he thought. She has brought a touch of spring into his life.

It was as well that there was happiness at Ellenhead that night. For elsewhere, in the capitals of Europe, men's minds reeled to a stunning shock.

In Paris that morning, the French Republic had cut off the French King's head.

"It means war, Catherine," Tristram told her when he heard the news. "It is now certain that France and England will soon be at war."

They looked anxiously at Stephen and saw by the pain in his eyes that he knew it, too.

With Uncle Fletcher's written permission and two plated candlesticks sent from Town End as a present, Catherine and Tristram were married at Ellenhead a month later. It was a simple wedding, without pomp. But it was hardly quiet, for the boys, given a half holiday for such a joyful event, lit a bonfire on the top of Ellencrag and set off rockets until far into the dusk.

A week later came the letter that sent Stephen out into the world again.

It was addressed to Tristram.

Catherine and Stephen, sitting with him at the breakfast table, saw with what eagerness he broke its seal and lost himself in its contents, and watched with growing curiosity as the expression on his face changed from one of affection to one of amusement and finally settled in a weary concern.

"Poor Joel," he sighed, putting the letter down. "He's always in trouble."

"Who's Joel?" asked Catherine. "A past pupil?"

"Joel Bankes? No. He's a scholar, a poet, and a prime begetter of crackpot ideas. We were friends at Balliol."

"I've never heard you talk about him," said Stephen.

"No. I guess you haven't."

After Oxford, he explained, their careers had led them along different paths. He—Tristram—had taken holy orders and had been appointed headmaster of Ellenhead Grammar School. Joel had become a Unitarian and had settled in Manchester.

"He was a Unitarian minister for a short time, but his ideas were too eccentric even for the Unitarians. Now he runs a school for poor children in the slums. He comes to me here every summer for a few days."

"And what's the new trouble he writes of?" asked Stephen, strangely intrigued by this odd friend from Tristram's past.

"Read his letter for yourself."

This is what Stephen read:

Manchester,
February 23rd, 1793

Dear Walkinshaw,

My congratulations, old friend, on the happy news of your marriage. I shall be coming north in the summer to pay my respects to your dear wife, but in the meantime pray give her my best wishes and warn her that as an old crony of her husband's I shall look for my seat in the inglenook.

You will, I trust, not be wearied with me for describing yet again what difficulties we meet with here in Manchester. More factories and mills spring up every month, and more blast furnaces belch their smoke, and every day more and more country folk come crowding into the town, looking for work. There are not enough houses for them, or schools, or places of worship—let alone enough drains, or fresh water, or green grass to refresh their souls. My poor children! They have so short a childhood here. Of harsh necessity, the parents are taking them from me even earlier than before so that they may earn their keep in the mills. Alas, we lack so many of the natural blessings of life. But, above all, Walkinshaw, we are short of men of good will in this dark and dreadful place. I speak with grief—for I have lost my good Francis Dove to a putrid fever. He died last week. I miss him sorely. He helped me in my ragged school and, moreover, visited the parents in our worst rookeries and slums.

I seek to replace this excellent young man. Have you a candidate for poverty, dirt, and no fame? I seek a fellow worker of courage and principles, *not* one full of religious cant. He must believe in the rights and dignity of the poorest and stupidest of mankind and must, my dear friend, share our conviction that those rights and dignities belong also to children. He must *love* them. I fear mine is a vain quest, and that I waste your time. I can offer only a low salary. But, should a past pupil or acquaintance of yours make such a venture, he shall have my friendship and a place in my home.

If you know of such a rash and unworldly young man, dear Walkinshaw, in God's name send him to me in haste.

Yours ever,
Joel Bankes.

"You see what I mean," said Tristram when Stephen had put down the letter. "Poor Joel, even at thirty-seven, still has his wagon hitched to the stars."

"What do you mean?"

"What young man in his senses would devote even a few years to so unpractical a cause?"

"Is it unpractical to teach the children of the poor?"

"No. If Joel could keep his pupils with him two years, three years . . . all well and good. But they are snatched from him before he has got them into their second readers. His is a hopeless task. Both his goodness and his learning are thrown away."

Stephen left the letter lying on the breakfast table and set off alone up Ellen Glen to think things out—for, in spite of Tristram's disparaging remarks, Joel Bankes and his crackpot school intrigued him. The prodigal idealism of both appealed to something buried deep in his nature.

But what about himself? Had he courage and principles? He doubted it. Did he really love small children? He did not know.

And yet . . . and yet . . . here was hope.

A traveler lost on a dark night will walk in the direction of a lighted window, however far away the cottage be, or faintly flickering the light.

"But, Stephen, you *can't* go," Catherine wept, when he told them his resolve. "Not to that dreadful place. You are not well enough. You need country air."

Francis Dove's untimely death filled her with fear for him.

"It's a waste of your gifts," protested Tristram, sick at heart to think that his best pupil was going the way of his best friend.

"*Gifts?*" Stephen burst out in bitterness. "What are these gifts? What good have they done either me or the world up to now?"

He set off for Manchester three weeks later—on the very day that
poor Mr. Fordwick threw away his crutch.

Tristram and Catherine stood at the door watching him striding away south, with the famous red-spotted bundle of clothes
swinging on the end of a hazel stick.

" 'Tomorrow to fresh Woods and Pastures new,' " murmured
Tristram sadly, half under his breath.

Catherine—taken up with her own sadness—failed to recog-
nize Stephen's favorite Milton. As she watched her brother go,
she knew that there was one last, urgent thing that she must say
to him before he was out of sight.

She ran after him, calling.

"Stephen," she panted, when she had caught up with him.
"Stephen . . . I wanted to say . . . we both wanted to say . . ."

He stopped, swung round, and looked down at her upturned
face.

". . . that Ellenhead . . . is always your home."

He nodded his head and smiled.

"If . . . if Manchester's no good," she pleaded, "come back
to us."

"You mean, if I make another mess of things," he said, grinning his old derisive grin.

Then—swept with an unwonted tenderness for her—he kissed
her quickly on the forehead and strode on.